Love is a Funny Thing

by

Trinity Johnson and Misty O'Neal

DORRANCE
PUBLISHING CO
EST. 1920
PITTSBURGH, PENNSYLVANIA 15238

The contents of this work, including, but not limited to, the accuracy of events, people, and places depicted; opinions expressed; permission to use previously published materials included; and any advice given or actions advocated are solely the responsibility of the author, who assumes all liability for said work and indemnifies the publisher against any claims stemming from publication of the work.

Dorrance Publishing Co
585 Alpha Drive
Suite 103
Pittsburgh, PA 15238
Visit our website at *www.dorrancebookstore.com*

ISBN: 978-1-6491-3460-8
eISBN: 978-1-6491-3813-2

Chapter 1

Blake

Love is a funny thing. We all think we know exactly what true love would feel like. In reality, we never know if the love we feel for a person is what true love actually feels like. In the moment of being with that person, it seems like the feelings we feel for them are at their extremes. We think that we can't feel any better than in that moment. The truth of the feeling love is that we will never understand what true love is. We are human, and in our brains, the one thing we love the most whether we realize it or not is ourselves. If it came down to saving someone else and saving ourselves, yes, some of us might choose to save the other person in that moment, but if we had to think about it, we would have to consider every option. I'm not saying that there aren't people who would risk their life for someone else; I am just saying that in order to do that, we have to truly love that person. Most people in their lifetime don't ever experience that type of love. My story is different though. My story is about a girl whose world was a rollercoaster.

My name is Blake Laurels. My childhood was not at all what you call ordinary. My mom took off on me, and after she did, I got abused by my father. When I was around 14, the government came to my house and took my father. They decided the best decision for me was to put me in the system. I have been moving from town to town ever since that day. I have lived in almost every state. This year's state will be Montana.

Since I moved there during the summer, I had a lot of time to get used to the surroundings. I got out of the car, and when I saw the house, it took my breath away. The house itself had so many windows... There had to at least be a hundred. There were 30 marble columns that went all the way up to the third floor. There were statues on both sides of the grand staircase that led up to the massive front porch. The house was painted a light sky blue, so if you were to look at it at the right angle, it would blend in with the sky. Waiting on the porch was a tall, dark-haired woman. Even from where I was standing, I could see the trauma and sadness in her ice-blue eyes. Next to her was a boy, very young and small. He had dark brown hair and black eyes that had no soul. To the right of the boy was a tall, well-built older boy. He had sandy brown hair and bluish-green eyes. When I looked into his eyes, I saw a hunger that was waiting to get out. The next person over was a man. Not a middle-aged man like the woman. The man was probably in his 70s and had grey hair that wasn't all there. His eyes were black and had experience but anger to them. He was the one that scared me the most.

Even though this family would probably be like all the others and get rid of me after a year, I had a feeling that the year I had ahead of me was going to last a lot longer than any other. I got to the porch, winded from the walk up the stairs, and all of them looked at me with no joy at all. They tried to put on a good show of happiness that I was there, but I knew better.

"Hi Blake, we are so glad to have you here," the woman said with no feeling in her voice.

"Thanks for having me," I tried to say in the kindest way I could. We walked through the enormous wooden door to the main room. The entryway was all-white with leather furniture and large arcs as walkways. The house was gorgeous. They helped me to my room, and I put up my belongings. The bedroom was beautiful. It had light grey curtains, and the bed sheets was light blue with grey trim. The bed was a huge, king size. Everything about this place reminded me of a fairytale, but fairytales aren't real.

An hour after putting up my things, they called me for dinner. I was walking through the multiple hallways. Before I knew it, I was lost. I tried to find my way back to my room, but when I turned around, there was a person right behind me. It was the little boy. He looked at me with those hurt and broken eyes. I was starting to get really faint.

"What's happening?"

He turned his head slightly to the side and said, "I'm sorry, but Mother told me not to say anything to you."

"Why are you doing to me!" I tried to turn and walk away, but when I tried to turn, I fell to the floor. My skull was starting to burn. It felt like my bones were tightening. The last thing I saw before blacking out was the older boy running and shaking the younger one.

I woke up in an unrecognizable bed. I woke with a jump. I got out of the bed and made a run for the door, but it was locked.

"I'm sorry for my little brother's manners," he said, rounding the corner as if it were the most ordinary thing in the world.

"What did he do to me?"

"He didn't do anything, you just fainted."

I knew that was a lie as soon as he said something.

"I know that's not true." He took a step closer, and I tried to step back, but I was already against the door. "Are you scared of me?" I knew he could sense my fear. Who wouldn't be scared when a little boy just knocked you out?

"N...No."

He laughed at that response, which just pissed me off rather than make me scared.

"I'm not scared of you, or your psychopath family." After I said that, I immediately regretted it. He took two steps and was right in front of me.

"You have no right to call the people that took you in psychos." I could practically feel the heat coming off of him. I looked in his sea blue eyes and saw a fire burning to get out. I saw myself in him. He then realized how close he had gotten and backed away.

"So, what's your story."

"My story? Which part, the part where my parents tortured me or the part where I got put into horrible homes?"

"How about we start with what you've done in the past year."

I hadn't really done anything in the past year. I was put through a lot of terrible stuff for the first few months, but other than that, I had just stayed in the foster home.

"I was in a horrible home for four months, then in the foster home for the next eight... Yeah, that's about it."

"What was so horrible about this home?"

"I... I'd rather not talk about it."

As I started to think about what happened that year, I could only remember the face of the person who both sexually and physically abused me.

The person I also killed. The boy looked at me with those piercing blue eyes, and I saw something that looked like compassion and worry.

"You don't have to tell me, I just wanted to know why my brother went after you."

"Wait, you mean there's a specific reason why he went after me, and it wasn't only because I was a new person?"

"My brother only goes after people who have something to fear or have done something worse than hitting someone. So, you must be really scared of someone in the house, or you've done something that you aren't telling me about and wasn't in your file." When he said that, a cold smile rose from his frown, and he got a twinkle in his eyes. He took steps forward, and I held my ground and looked directly into his eyes, mentally telling him to back the hell up.

"See, my brother feeds on bad memories or fear. Do you know what I feed on?" I gulped and started breathing unevenly.

"No!"

The grin was still on his face, but his eyes had changed, and I am not talking about the look in his eyes; I am talking about the color. His blue-ish green eyes changed to yellowish green.

"I feed off of good memories and confusion."

He lifted his head and sniffed the air as if smelling for his next meal. I turned and tried the door handle, but as I turned, he grabbed my wrist and pushed me against the door.

"You smell like an appetizer."

"Let me go NOW!"

He jumped back, and his eyes changed back.

"How did you do that?"

"How did I hurt you, how did I make you believe that I didn't know what was happening? Well, that's the easy part. See, the first people who took me in were the same thing as you are, Jackson."

I felt a smile appear on my face. He had no idea who I was or what I could do.

"Ho…"

"How did I know your name? You really think that I would be that easily manipulated. I will let you and your family live as long you can prove that you aren't the same as the others that I have met."

His face changed from the deviant smile to a frown that looked intrigued. I could see in his eyes that I wasn't the first one to know what he was. He was... intrigued.

"Get that look and thought out of your head, I'm not letting you live because I have feelings for you. The only reason I'm doing this is because I don't want to be quick to judge someone for what others have done." I turned and walked out of the door with a devilish smile.

I didn't like to kill people, but I enjoy knowing that they won't be able to hurt anyone else. Tricking him into believing that I didn't know what was happening made me feel a little guilty; the hardest thing to do was to fake not being able to open the door. He had put some of the energy from someone's happy memories on the door handle, so unless you were happy or comfortable, you couldn't enter or exit the room. It was hard to make it seem like I was scared of him. I knew he could read my emotions. I knew all of them could. His brother, though, I didn't expect one of them so young to be able to take that much energy from me. The family is strong; I can sense that. The oldest a child who has that power that I have seen before was almost 16, but that child was barely nine years of age. I walked back to my room. When I entered the room, a maid was standing there. The maid had grayish-blonde hair and greyish-blue eyes that had absolutely no emotion in them.

"Dinner has already started, ma'am, the master and mistress would like to know if you will be joining then."

"Excuse me for asking but, how old are you?"

"I am 22 years old. Why do you ask?"

"How long have you been with this family?"

"For almost three years. I still don't understand what this has to do with dinner."

"Sorry, no, I will not be joining them for dinner, I am a little tired from the ride."

The maid started walking towards the door, unaffected by my choice.

"Umm, what's your name by the way?" I asked in the politest way I could.

"Thalia, Thalia Jones."

She exited the room with a little bit of happiness in her eyes. It upset me terribly; the family or someone in the family had been feeding off of her happy memories and her emotions. I would not allow any more of this feeding on innocent people! I hoped that Jackson told everyone in his family what we had discussed. The family would most likely try to take me on, all of them against me, but if they did, I would explain to them why that not such a good idea. I had to deal with that happening once before, but they didn't stand much of a chance. See, in order for them to live and use their abilities, they have to have a constant supply of emotion or memories with correspond with their gifts. Most of their kind live in very populated areas, so they can feed off people's emotions.

This family, though, they were going to be tough to figure out. I knew that the children tried to act like normal people, and they went to school, but they went to private school. It was probably about nine o'clock at night. The day was ending, and I was so relieved that it was. It had been a long day, and there were many more to come as long as this family decided to change their ways. For the first time in a long time, I finally found a family that might be able to pass the test.

I woke up to yelling and Thalia talking to someone in the hallway.

"Sir, I didn't say anything to the girl about what you and your family are I swear."

"You shouldn't swear, Thalia, it's not very respectful. What's that smell? I smell is that worry coming from you, or is it anger?"

"I... I don't have any emotions, remember? Your family made sure to drain them from me."

"Yes, I remember, but maybe that girl has given you ideas or even worse, hope that you could be the way you were before you came here."

"Sir, I know that one girl is not going to bring back the hope and emotions that your family took from me years ago."

"Careful. You don't want to let that anger that is boiling in you to be seen by my wife. She might get hungry. We may have taken enough emotion from you to last us four years, but we can always take more. The more we take, the more powerful we get and that is always enough motive to drain you again."

What? How was that possible? Until now, the only ones that I have faced could only syphon enough energy for, at most, a year. This family must have been doing this for a very long time for them to be able to syphon that much. I wonder if the child could syphon that much.

"I can sense the hope inside your heart, and I am getting hungry. You're lucky that it's not enough to equal a year, or I would take it right now."

I stepped outside of the room and into the hallway. The man, or Casey, which was his original name, looked amused that had overheard them, as if he knew I was there the whole time

"Leave her alone. You have no right to feed off of an innocent person."

"You're a brave girl, you know that," he said in a mocking voice. He gently brushed a finger across the scar on my eyebrow. "You fought so long and hard. Maybe it's about time you stop fighting and listen." He grabbed my face with one hand and lifted it up where I was looking at the ceiling. "You have so much hope that we will be good people. Your emotions are strong and smell so good."

"Get away from me. If you don't want to get hurt, you better back off."

"I heard about the trick you pulled on my son. I am a lot older and stronger than him, so go ahead and try it."

"Back OFF!"

I tried to use his abilities against him like I did with Jackson, but without knowing what his abilities were, I couldn't use that. I was going to have to get rid of all emotions to get out of his grasp.

"It's funny that you think that you can do that. You see, Miss Laurels, you can't simply just get rid of hope." He said that with humor. And with that information I knew exactly what his ability was. His ability is strength and getting in their head. I used the power I had to hurt him.

And with that, I did it. He jumped back in pain screaming. His hand steaming and sizzling.

"What did you do?" He looked at me with confusion, pain, and anger.

"Careful, your wife might smell your anger and frustration. You shouldn't take me so lightly. I might be a teenage girl, but I am not someone who is new to your kind."

"You spoiled little…"

"Watch yourself. You should be careful about your next words." When I said that, he looked at me with realization in his eyes.

"I know what you are."

"Good, then you know not to mess with me. There will not be any more draining Thalia. If you have enough to last four years, then that's how long you will wait to drain anyone ever again. You will not feed off of any innocent people. If you need to feed, you ask me, or you go and find a person who deserves that. Do we have an understanding?"

He nodded his head letting me know that he understood completely.

"Good, you will also tell your entire family. If any of them step out of line more than five times or try to fight me, then I will have no choice but to either lock them up or end them. I will give the child more chances than the rest of you, but I do expect everyone to know what will happen."

I really hoped they will understand and change their ways. After that dramatic turn of events, I went straight to bed.

The morning sun blinded my eyes as I woke up. It must have been at least five in the morning. School started at eight, and of course, it is a private school that ends at three and doesn't have summers. So, no getting used to this place. I got up and went to my closet. I had to wear a uniform (of course). The uniform had a white blouse, black and green checkered skirt that only went down a little below the middle of my thigh, a green jacket, black heels, and a tie. I threw my burning red hair into a braid and brushed my teeth. I needed to ask Jackson if the school had any normal people going there. I would need to figure out where he was first.

I put on my uniform and started walking down stairs. I smelt burning bacon from the kitchen. The whole family was in the kitchen eating breakfast, but as soon as I walked in, they all turned in looked in my direction with anger in their eyes.

"Good morning everyone. Jackson, can I talk to you for a minute?"

"Sure," he said with worry in his voice. We walked in the hallway and stood by the door.

"So, are there any people like me that go to your school?"

"I think there are three, but they are mostly for us to feed off of. Don't get mad or worry; they volunteered."

"Okay, so basically everyone is going to look at me like a snack. Awesome." I couldn't imagine what I was going to be treated like at this school, but I did know that I couldn't find out all of their abilities in one day. If they all decided to feed on me at once, I wouldn't stand a chance.

"You don't have to worry about that, you know," he said with kindness in his voice.

"Why not?"

"As long as you stay by my side, no one will even think about touching you." He looked at me with admiration in his eyes. No one had ever looked at me like that before, let alone one of them. I expected hate or dislike, but not admiration or sympathy. I could feel my face heating.

"You're not like the rest of your family, are you?"

"I feed off of good memories mostly, so of course I care about people more than the rest of them, plus I happen to actually like your confidence, unlike the rest of them." He looked into my eyes and made me feel something that I had never felt before. My heart actually skipped a beat, and I felt comfortable around him even though I knew I shouldn't. How could someone change so quickly?

"Don't forget that I can hear your thoughts," he said with amusement in his voice. He smiled with confidence. My face started to burn with redness even more.

"Stay out of my head! You will know when I want you to hear me." He still kept a grin on his face.

"It's not like I am choosing what I hear. You are going to have to keep your thoughts clear at school, or everyone is going to hear what you think of them."

"You could just expand your barrier with me, but then you would use your energy."

I thought about this for a minute. I really need to be able to think about things at school, like figuring out everyone's abilities and doing school work. If I even think one thing, people will be able to get into my head, and I am not willing to let them find out that my intentions are not to be friends or that I know what they are. That will cause chaos, and I will never be trusted by any of them.

"If you share your barrier... I... I will give you some of my energy and emotion." His face told me everything I needed to know. That even though he was surprised by my offer, he wasn't going to give up the chance to feed. "Do we have a deal?"

"Yes." We shook hands, and a moment later Julie walked in. She had a look of disgust in her eyes. She looked back and forth between me and Jackson.

"Are you giving *her* a ride to school, or is she staying here with your father and me?"

When she thought of me staying with them, a devilish smile played across her face.

"Yes, Mother, I am, and no, I will not let her stay in this house alone with you or Father. I do not trust you to be in a room alone with her." He looked at his mother with confidence and defiance.

"Why are you protecting her, son? She has threatened your only family and you choose to protect her." She had such anger in her voice that I felt it was a little unnerving since I didn't know her ability, and I couldn't fight against her in any way if she wanted to she could hurt me. "Whatever, just leave already," she said as she turned and walked away.

Jackson hurried me out the door and to the car. He immediately started the car and sped out of the drive way down the road.

"Look, I'm sorry about my mother and how she acted. I would say she's not usually like that, but I would be lying. She doesn't like the fact that you are the only person that could hurt us if you find anything out about us, and she doesn't like you threatening her."

"I won't try to hurt any of you as long as I don't have a reason to."

After that conversation, he turned on the radio and just drove. When we left the house, it was six-thirty, and when we arrived at the school, it was seven-thirty. We got out of the car, and I quickly noticed that everyone was looking at me with confusion, and some even with hunger. I guess that some of them fed off of confidence. Others most likely off of unsureness, but as soon as they realized I was walking with Jackson, they all looked away as if they feared him. I looked up at him, and I realized that he held himself like he owned the place. I wonder if he actually did. I soon realized that I needed to make sure that the barrier was on me.

"Did you already spread your barrier?"

He laughed at my question.

"Of course I have, but that won't stop them from knowing or smelling that your normal."

"So, at lunch there is normal food, right?"

He looked down as if he had to think of that question.

"Actually, no there isn't any human food."

"Umm, what am I supposed to eat then?" His face contorted into a frown and his right eyebrow started twitching. He looked at me with concern.

"You need to hide your hunger at lunch as well as you can because the only person that feeds on that emotion happens to be the only person as powerful as me." He had so much worry in his voice that I even started to worry.

"Wait, do you know their abilities, because if you do, then they won't be able to syphon from me."

"His ability is that he is able to either make them fall in love or make them hate anyone of his choice." As soon as heard that, my heart stopped for a second, and I stopped walking. He stopped and turned to look at me. I wasn't sure if I would be able to control him because if he made me fall in love with him before I realized that he was doing it, then I wouldn't want to hurt him.

"I won't let that happen." I kept forgetting that he was hearing my thoughts. Why does he care so much whether or not I get hurt or something happens to me anyway? I threatened his family and hurt him, so why would he care?

"I trust you." I looked him straight in the eyes as I said it.

"Don't worry too much he has to actually say that he wants you to fall in love with that person to make it happen, so you will know when he is doing it." I started to walk again.

As we entered the building, I saw a crowd of people standing around a locker looking at something. No not something, someone. It was a girl about my age being syphoned by a boy about Jackson's age. I ran over there as fast as I could and stepped right in between the boy and the girl, knocking the boys hand away from the girl.

"Leave her alone."

"Look at that, a human that has the guts to say something," he said looking at the other girls who were too scared to do anything and started laughing.

"Don't start anything, Lucian!" Jackson said as he stood by my side.

"I am not afraid of you like everyone else, Jackson, I will start anything I want." He grinned mischievously.

"Well, that was a lot easier to find you than I thought it was going to be. You came straight into my hands." I laughed as I said it. He turned back to me with anger in his eyes.

"You have no idea who you're dealing with, little girl." He was right; I was a lot shorter than him. I was standing at 5'3" and him at 6'4", but it didn't make a difference to me.

"It's funny you think that you said a chance against me," I said with confidence. I could see the anger and curiosity on his face. He took steps closer to me. I held my ground in front of the nearly drained girl, and I could tell he expected me to be scared.

"I said to back off." This time, when I said the words, he dropped to his knees in agony and pain. He must have been extremely powerful because the stronger the person, the more it hurts.

"What are you doing to me!"

"Teaching you manners and your place. When it comes to these girls, or any girl, you are to treat them with kindness and respect, do you understand?"

"Rot in hell." I pushed a little more effort into my power over him. His hair and clothes started to steam, and he screamed out in pain.

"Do you understand?" I repeated the question. He was kneeled over in agony.

"Y…Yes ma'am" Struggling to say the words through his teeth.

"Good, we have an understanding." I turned to walk away and saw everyone staring with awe in their eyes and horror on their faces. I looked at Jackson who until now hadn't seen what my powers could do to someone that strong. I walked through the crowd of people, seeing some of the teachers. They even looked scared of me. I could hear Jackson's footsteps behind me. We turned the corner and ended up in an unoccupied hallway.

"Hey, umm, are you okay."

"Yeah, I'm fine, why?" I couldn't understand why he would think that there was something wrong with me. Then it hit me—a wave of exhaustion. As soon as the feeling hit me, my legs gave out. I fell right into Jackson's arms, and he carried me to a room. I'm guessing that it was the nurse's office because it had beds and dividers. He laid me down on one of the beds and sat in a chair next to me.

"How did you know that would happen?" I was confused as to how he could know.

"Please stop being so confused." I forgot that he fed off of confusion.

"I…I'm sorry. Just answer the question." He tried to cover his nose to stop smelling the confusion.

"I could feel your strength failing, that's all."

"I don't know why that happened."

"You have probably never controlled someone that strong or for that long." I tried to stay conscious and awake, but as my mind kept questioning things, I kept getting mentally weaker. I could tell that the smell of my confusion was driving him crazy. I finally blacked out from exhaustion.

Chapter 2

Jackson

The smell of her confusion was still stuck in my head. She looked so beautiful when she slept. The innocent look on her face made me forget that there was a powerful and dangerous person in the girl lying fast asleep. How could a human be so powerful? Then it hit me. Why didn't I realize it before; she didn't have any real powers. The only way she was able to hurt us was she was using her willpower to burn the mental connection our kind have to everyone. In order to use our abilities, we have to use our mental hearing to connect with the person we are using them on. She was using her willpower to block whoever was trying to use their abilities, and it hurt the person doing it.

In the moment, I noticed that Blake was dreaming of something. My mental barrier was allowing me to see what she is dreaming about. She was talking to some woman, no not talking yelling at her.

"I can't believe that you would leave me alone with that monster of a father!" she yelled at her mother.

"I never cared about you, I just had you to make him happy, but then he started to care about you more than he cared about me." The way this woman was talking to her was making my blood boil. I knew it was just a dream so, why was I getting so upset?

"You know you shouldn't invade her personal space. She might just snap on you." I turned to look at who was talking. Sitting on one of the beds with ice on his head was Lucian.

"You know, if you would have just backed down and listened, she wouldn't have hurt you that much." I tried to sound sure about that, but to be honest, I didn't even know if she would have hurt him more or not.

"I didn't think that such a small little human could have that much will power."

"Yeah, neither did I." I looked at Blake, taking in all of her features. She had a little scar on her right eyebrow that I just noticed. I would ask her how she got it, but I didn't want to pry.

"She was a very interesting girl."

"If I were you, I would keep my distance Lucian."

"I know. You might want to keep her close to you. I have heard people talking about trying to get rid of her because they are worried about how she will affect the way they live."

"Yes, I figured as much. She has already warned my family about what will happen if we don't change our ways. She even fought my father. He said it was the worst pain he has felt."

"She is very confusing. I do have one question though."

"Go ahead, ask."

"How does your family keep from feeding off of her? I know that your family feeds off of almost every emotion. It must be extremely hard for your mom, considering that she feeds off of anger and confidence."

"No, it's not that difficult, but I guess I can't speak for all of my family. I am worried though. Blake doesn't know what my mother's abilities are so, if my mom attacks her, she won't be able to stop her."

"Can't you just tell her what your mother's abilities are?"

"I'm afraid not. None of my family except my father know what they are."

"I don't mean to sound like I am trying to try anything with he,r but if your family does try to hurt her, she could always just stay at my house. I live on my own after all, and I am hardly ever home. You could come and visit and stay some days. It's just a suggestion."

"Why are you willing to help her? She just nearly put you into a coma?"

"I don't know. When I was trying to get into her head and she used her willpower, I felt the emotion she was using to keep me out. I felt the emotion, and something in my head became protective over her."

"That's what happened to me when she used her willpower to keep me out." There was something about this girl that is changing the way someone feels towards everyone. The power she had over me and Lucian wasn't just physical, it was emotional. The only problem was that she didn't know the power she held on us.

"I don't know if she would be comfortable with that idea," I tried to explain to him.

"Yeah, you're probably right."

"What is he doing here?" I turned to look at Blake, who was wide awake. She was staring at Lucian with confusion and anger.

"I kinda had to get my mental hearing and link checked out after you burned me." He looked at Blake as if she had done something wrong. I could tell that Blake did not want to talk to him after the events that went on today. I got up and walked toward Lucian and pulled the divider all the way closed.

"Look, Lucian, I think it might be best if you leave her alone for the day," I whispered to him.

"Okay, but just this once, Jakson." Lucian exited the room and shut the door. I turned back around and sat down in the chair next to Blake. She had turned over on her side and was grabbing her head in pain.

"Hey, are you okay?" She didn't look at me instead she tried to stand up. Instead, she fell on the floor.

"I... I can't see anything, my head is spinning, and I can't move my legs." Blake was lying on the floor suppressing a scream. My mental connection that I had with her was burning up. I couldn't see what was happening. It would take someone stronger than me to see what was wrong, and there was only one person that was nearby who was stronger than me. I ran out into the hall and saw him turn the corner. I sprinted after him.

"Lucian!" He turned to look at me.

"What?"

"You have to come. There is something wrong with Blake." As soon as I said that, he went racing down the hall towards the nurse's room. We got inside and went over to where Blake was lying on the floor.

"What's wrong with her?" The amount of concern in his voice was strange.

"I don't know. I am not strong enough to see inside her head." I let go of my mental barrier that was stopping Lucian from seeing inside of her head.

"Blake, you have to let me see what's wrong." She was blocking him out of her head without my help. I could tell that it was hurting her even more to use her own willpower as a mental barrier. She was too exhausted to do that;

the strength to keep him out was too much. She fainted from the use of her trying to keep him out. I guess he finally got into her head because he quit talking and just stared at her.

"Her brain was put through too much strain. Basically, she doesn't have enough strength to keep her body functioning; her brain is shutting itself down, and if we can't stop it, she will not live."

My heart started racing, and I couldn't believe that the first day she was here and she was already in a live or die situation.

"How do we help her?"

"We can't. The only thing we can do is go inside her head and encourage her to pull through, but the rest is up to her."

"You're the only one of us that can get in her head." I didn't have enough power to be completely in her head.

"I can give you some of my power to use to get inside." The idea of him giving me some of his power made me feel weak. I knew I couldn't repay the gesture, but the idea of him being in her head alone was unsettling.

"Okay." I felt a sudden surge of energy, and the next thing I knew I was inside Blake's head seeing everything she was.

We were in a small room that had cracked walls and ceiling. There was a brown worn blanket on a sleeping bag on the floor. The room had no windows, no other furniture, and no color. I heard yelling outside the door. It sounded like a younger girl and an older woman. Lucian and I walked down the stairs and into an even smaller living room. There was a glass and metal table, a red couch, a small box TV, and a brown rug. The living room looked exactly like the room upstairs except with more furniture and color. It was clear that only two people were supposed to live in the house, but it looked like more than five had been living here. The trash was overflowing with garbage, there was stains all over the rug, and the couch was worn down to the springs.

The woman was about 5'6", muscular, with short brown hair, black eyes, and a crooked smile. She and Blake were standing in the middle of the room next to the table.

"You ungrateful little tramp!" the woman was yelling at Blake.

"I'm sorry," Blake was crying.

"You will be, all you do is eat my food and take my money; you don't even have any emotions that I need."

"What are you talking about?" This must have been before Blake knew about us. Blake was so confused. The woman got even more angry with her. Before I realized what happened next, the woman pushed Blake. Blake landed on the table. When she hit the table, it collapsed inward and fell to pieces.

"Now you're breaking my furniture." The woman jumped onto Blake grabbed a piece of glass and cut Blake across the eyebrow. I finally understood where the scar came from.

"Get off!" Blake let out a scream, and the woman fell over next to her, clenching her head. Blake kept pushing for the woman to hurt. I blinked, and the woman was dead. Blake was shivering, just sitting there letting the blood run down her face. I wanted to run over and comfort her. I wanted to make the pain stop, but as much as I wanted to, I couldn't touch her.

The setting changed, and we were standing in a huge house. It looked surprisingly familiar. The walls were white and a little too perfect. Actually, the whole house was a little too perfect. Everything was white, there wasn't a single smudge or stain in the whole house. We walked around and found a room that had a door that was made of steel and heavily secure. The only thing it wasn't was sound proof. I could hear the sobs coming from the room. We somehow managed to get into the room.

Sitting in the middle of a padded white room was Blake. Someone had put her in a straitjacket. The door clicked and opened. A middle-aged man entered. He looked like my dad except for his eyes, which were dark brown. Suddenly, I remembered the house; it was my uncle's house. What was Blake doing here? I didn't remember her ever being here. I guess I didn't really get to see her because she was in this room. It would make sense, now that I thought about it. My uncle died about three years ago because of a hunter, but I never imagined that the hunter could have been Blake. There was the possibility that it was another hunter, but it was highly unlikely.

"Blake, please just give me access to your mind, and then I will let you go."

"Never! You'll have to kill me first," she said as she spit at him. Why would my uncle need access to her mind? Was there something valuable that she was hiding from him? Lucian walked up to Blake.

"Blake, you need to wake up! If you don't snap out of it, you'll die."

"L...Lucian? What are you doing in my head?"

"I'm sorry, Blake, but you're dying. Your mind is shutting itself down." Blake's facial expression changed to worry and realization.

"Are you sure about this?" Her eyes screamed for it not to be real.

"I'm sorry, but yes we are sure." I couldn't believe she had to deal with this many of our kind and has never gone through this.

"Blake, the only way you are going to be able to get through this is if you shut off your mind enough to where it has time to regain your strength." She nodded her head letting us know that she understood, but she looked like she was in shock from finding this out.

After we got out of her head, she finally got her mind to turn off.

"How does someone with her amount of willpower and experience with our kind not go through this all the time?" I was looking at Blake when I said it, but Lucian knew I was asking him.

"Honestly, she might just be experiencing emotions for the first time since she has started dealing with our kind. Having to keep her emotions hidden from everyone she is around was so easy. Letting out her emotions, even a little, must have confused her mentally and stressed her out."

"Why would she have to keep her emotions locked up? Actually I have never met a human who could keep their emotions locked up." I had never met a human that hunted my kind either, so why was her locking up her emotions such a surprise to me? Lucian looked up at me, and I could see the worry in his eyes. I knew he cared as much as I did for her safety.

"I don't know how she does it. I haven't ever met a human who could hurt me the way she did. She's very unique."

Lucian left the nurse's room and headed back to class. The day was almost over, and Blake was still asleep. I looked over at the other beds. They looked so comfortable. I knew that it was going to be awhile before Blake woke up, so what was the harm in sleeping a little? I laid down on the bed that was surprisingly not as comfortable as it looked, but it was better than nothing. After lying there for a few moments, I finally managed to fall asleep.

I had a dream about what I had seen in Blake's head that day. About all of the horrible people that hurt her in so many ways. Also about how it might be possible that my uncle or my parents could be hiding something from me and the fact that Blake was the key to whatever they needed. I woke up in a cold sweat. I looked across the room where Blake was now sitting up, knees against her chest, thinking about something. She looked so scared but also like she was in deep thought. Maybe thinking about what had happened today and the fact that today might have been her last. She noticed that I had gotten up and was looking at her.

"Your mom called. Don't worry I told her that you fell asleep in the nurse's office and that we would head home as soon as you awake." The fact that my mom actually believed her or even talked to her surprised me.

"Thank you." I was still trying to comprehend what all of this meant. Did my parents just adopt her, hoping that she didn't know who or what they were, just so they could get the information my uncle didn't acquire? I don't even know which is the truth and which is the lie.

"Blake, can I ask you a question about what I saw in your head?" Her expression changed back to her normal look of neutral.

"If you're going to ask me about your uncle, you're wasting our time. I won't say anything about that."

"Blake, he was my uncle. I have a right to know what happened and what he wanted." I could feel the anger coming off of her. I didn't need any special powers to do that.

"You wanna know what happened, okay, I will tell you. Your uncle wanted something I couldn't and wouldn't give to him. He wouldn't leave me alone, so I killed him, that's what happened." I can't believe the amount of courage she had to say that to me. After I just saved her life, she wanted to get all defensive and tell me off. The rage I was feeling clouded my vision, and before I realized, I blacked out.

I woke up on the floor of my room. I had blood on my hands, but no memory of whose it was. It couldn't have been mine because I didn't have a cut or anything that it could have come from. I hoped it wasn't Blake's. I really didn't want it to be hers; if it was I don't know if she would ever trust me again.

"Blake! Blake, please answer me!"

"I'm here." Her voice was coming from the bathroom. I went to open the door and found it locked.

"Blake, is everything okay? Are you hurt? Please answer me or unlock the door." I had never been so worried about someone before.

"I...I will be fine, I just have a little scratch. I can't unlock the door because, I can't walk to the door." Something in my gut was telling me that something was wrong, and it was my fault.

"Wh...Why? What's wrong?"

"My leg is ripped open."

"How did it happen?" I was so worried that she was going to say that I had attacked her or nearly killed her.

"After you got mad, you went running down the hall looking for someone to feed off of. I went after you, but I couldn't find you. Instead of finding you, I found a group of people standing in the hall. They all wore blue jean jackets with a tiger on the back. I guess they saw me as a threat or thought I overheard something, but they attacked me. I couldn't keep them all away because I didn't know any of their abilities." Something in me was relieved, but at the same time, I was worried. I might not have been the one that hurt her, but someone else would now, and she was still hurt.

"Okay, don't worry, I will find a way to get the door open." I had to figure out how to calm down to get the door open.

"Why don't you just take the spell off the door?" She had a good idea, the only problem with that is in order to do that I would have to know how.

"Yeah, umm… About that."

"You don't know how, do you?"

"No." I felt so embarrassed. How could I use an ability and not know how to reverse it? Blake could die because my dumb ass was being stupid and careless. Who even needs a spell like that on a bathroom door that locks?

"Okay, I am going to try to calm down enough to open the door. I need you to keep talking to me Blake."

"I have stopped the bleeding as much as I can. I shouldn't pass out, so you don't have to worry." This fact didn't bring much comfort, but at least I knew she had stopped the bleeding enough to the point that I didn't have to rush myself to get the door open.

"Okay, just stay awake and respond when I talk to you." I went to the middle of my room and tried to get myself to calm down. How was I supposed to calm down when Blake was bleeding to death, and I couldn't even open a door? I looked around the room and saw a picture of Philip and me at the lake. Of course! Philip could take away my fear. I didn't know if it would work, but I have to try.

I ran down the hall toward Philip's room. He was sitting in the middle of his room, playing with a toy train. He wasn't smiling or frowning. His face was expressionless. Sometimes, I didn't even know if he was the slightest bit human or if he even had emotions.

"Philip, Blake is in trouble. I need you to come to my room and help me. Do you understand?" He nodded his head up and down slowly then got up and started walking down the hall with his toy train in his hand. I couldn't make him walk any faster than he was, so I decided to go make sure that Blake was still awake and breathing. I ran back down the hall to my room. The door must have shut when I went out of the room because when I got there the door was closed, and I couldn't get in until Philip got down the hall to the room. Philip was barely halfway here.

"Blake, can you hear me? Are you still awake? Please say something," I yelled at the top of my voice.

"Jackson." Her voice was getting weaker. Even through the door, I could hear that she was losing consciousness. I had almost lost her once today. Philip finally got to the room and opened the door for me and then walked to the bathroom door and opened it.

"Thank you, Philip!" I hugged him and then ran into the bathroom. Blake was sitting in the bottom of the shower. Her leg and arm were tied with two pieces of shirt that she had torn from her uniform. There was blood trailing through the bathroom and on the walls of the shower.

"Blake, I am going to carry you to the car. Then I am getting you to the hospital. I don't care what my parents say. I am not letting you die." She snickered at that comment.

"That's funny considering that when I got home today and was bleeding, I told them that I needed to go to the hospital, and they put me in the bathroom. They shut the door and tried to make it look like it was your fault. You really think they are going to let you save my life?"

I was speechless how could my parents not care what happens to people. I can slightly understand, considering that Blake threatened my parents, but no one deserves to die, especially not like that.

Carrying Blake down the stairs, I realized that she was strangely light. I wasn't saying that she was usually heavy, but I knew that she wasn't supposed to feel so easy to carry. She had lost so much blood that she was now pounds lighter. I made it down the stairs and started walking towards the door. A few feet away from the door, my mother was holding a knife. She was sharpening it and looking at me for the first time with hate in her eyes. Then I looked at the knife and saw that it had blood on it. The thought of my mother even touching Blake with the knife was enough to make my blood boil.

"You should have left her to die," my mother said, looking at the blood on the knife with humor.

"What kind of person would I be if I did? Wait, I know the answer to that question. I would be like the rest of you—a murder."

My mom's face turned red with rage and embarrassment.

"You shouldn't talk to me like I am a killer. The only reason I am doing this is to protect our family and our legacy. You really think that I would just let that girl come in and threaten us?"

How could I be a child of such a monster? She wasn't worried about me or the family; the only thing she was worried about was her pride.

"Whatever, Mother! Move away from the door. I am taking her to the hospital."

"I can't let you do that, Jackson. She cannot be allowed to live. She has shamed this family and has hunted our entire family line. She killed your grandpa, grandma, cousins, and most recently your uncle."

My mom had to be lying. I looked down at Blake, who was slowly starting to lose consciousness and turn pale. I knew about my uncle, so that didn't surprise me but, I couldn't believe that Blake, this girl who had opened herself up and nearly died to help me, could do that. Sure, she had the power to do it, but I couldn't believe it; no, I won't accept it. The rage was starting to make my vision blur at this point. If I didn't get Blake out of here, then she was going to die.

"I don't care what you have to say, Mother. I won't let her die."

My mom started laughing.

"Isn't that cute? You've started to care for this girl even though she nearly killed you." She started to move away from the door with a crooked smile on her face.

"Okay, I will let you save her. Not because I want her to live, but because I want her to break your heart, so you kill her. Then you will unlock your full potential." I could hear the amusement and curiosity in her voice. I walked past her and out the door. I was looking for the car and saw that it had been ran into the mailbox. My dad was standing outside the car with the keys in his hand and a grin on his face.

"You're not going anywhere, son." My father thought that I was going to take that car but, it was my turn to outsmart him and my mom.

"You're right, I'm not going anywhere in that car." I pulled the truck keys out of my pocket and walked to the barn, where I had parked it in case of emergencies. The barn was old and broken down. No one had used it for anything more than storage since the 90s. The truck that I had put in there had been in there since my last birthday, and I told my parents that I had drove it into a lake. They never questioned it because I told them that it was my first vehicle and that it was their fault for having high expectations.

The truck wasn't locked, so I opened the door and set Blake down in the passenger seat. My father was standing in the doorway of the barn with the shotgun in hand.

"Father, please just let me go and take care of her."

His face was calm and relaxed and then he started laughing.

"You think I was going to use this on her? No, son, this is for you to use on your mother if she tries to stop you from getting her to the hospital." I was extremely confused. Why would my dad want to help me take care of Blake or even care emotionally for her?

"I want you to start making choices for yourself, and today, you showed me that you cared so much for Blake that you would disobey your mother. That's enough to prove to me that you can make your own choices."

The roads were a little slick because it had rained earlier, but I didn't care I had to get Blake to the hospital, even if it meant risking my own skin. I began to realize that even if I did get Blake to the hospital in time, where would she go? I couldn't ask her to go back to the house with the woman who tried to kill her. The only way I was going to let her go back to the house was if she knew my mother's abilities, so she could defend herself. I could call Lucian and ask if he could take her to his house, but then again, I didn't really trust him with her, especially when she wasn't able to fight him off. I was about to start thinking of other places she could go when an idea popped into my head.

I called Lucian and told him to meet us at the hospital. I looked over at Blake and I could definitely see the scar on her eyebrow now that the blood was drying. We finally got to the hospital, and Lucian was already there.

"Lucian, go inside and tell them we have an emergency and need help." Lucian took off towards the doors and was yelling for help while I was getting Blake out of the car. By the time Blake was out of the car and halfway to the door, the doctors came running out with a stretcher ready to take her inside. They took her to the emergency room and left me to explain what happened to Lucian.

"I leave you two alone for two hours, and one of you ends up almost dead!" I could tell that he was on the verge of losing it.

"She got jumped by the Blue Tiger Gang. Also, my mom tried to kill her when she found out she was hurt and I was unconscious." I tried to make it not sound as bad as it was, but I could see from his facial expression that he was getting confused.

"Wait, why would your mom want to kill Blake?" I looked away from Lucian's eyes to the floor.

"Maybe because Blake threatened our family and killed some of my other family." His eyes got wide with amazement and curiosity. "It's a long story," I told him, hoping that he might understand.

"Now, are you going to tell me how we are going to prevent her from seeing your mother again?" Lucian said with determination. I was about to tell him my idea to keep Blake safe from my mother when a nurse came running out.

"Are either of you related to the girl that we just came in? She lost a lot of blood, and we need a transfer ASAP." My eyes widened. As far as I knew, Blake didn't have any family. Being what I was, I could give her my blood because our blood could change to what we wanted it to be depending on our abilities.

Chapter 3

Lucian

Jackson was relatively calm considering everything that had happened to him in the 24 hours. He was now asleep on the couch they had in the waiting room. He had just given the doctors an excessive amount of blood to make sure that Blake would make it through to see tomorrow. He didn't get to tell me what the idea for keeping Blake safe was, but to be honest, as long as she was safe, I would be fine with whatever the plan was. For some reason, the feelings I had for Blake hadn't gone away. Usually when started to feel the slightest hint of emotion for someone, especially a girl, the feeling would be gone in about a day.

I started drifting off to sleep around one in the afternoon the next day; I hadn't slept all night while I was waiting on Blake's conditions. I was almost asleep when the doctor started walking my way.

"Are you here for Miss Laurels?"

He looked at me with half-consciousness.

"Yes, me and the guy sleeping on the couch over by the wall. Why? Is she okay?"

"She's fine; she has just lost a lot of blood and tore her leg up extremely bad."

"Okay, so when can we take her home?"

"It's going to be at least 24 hours until we release her from the critical care." My head was hurting from staying up all night, and the news about Blake having to be in this place for even longer didn't help.

"Thank you for letting us know," Jackson said from the couch where he was now sitting with his elbows on his knees. We quit asking questions and let the doctor get back to her job.

After the doctor was out of earshot, I started to ask about the plan.

"Do you think that it would be okay if Blake and myself could stay at your place until it's safe for her at my house?" Jackson asked as if he was scared of the answer.

I started laughing.

"Of course you can, why did you think I would ever say no to that kind of question? You and Blake are always welcome."

Jackson got such a big grin on his face that I didn't know if he could see through the smile.

We finally got to see Blake. She was lying in the hospital bed in her hospital gown. She looked like she had just woken up from a good night's rest. Her hair was in a cute messy bundle, and her face had a cute yet not fully-awake calmness to it. She was beautiful, even when she didn't realize it. Of course, when Jackson walked in, he ran to her side as if he was her superhero. I rolled my eyes at the thought of that.

"Hey, Jackson. Lucian! What are you doing here? I thought y'all went home." She was still sleepy, and probably still had a little bit of the medicine they gave her to make the pain go away in her system, but it didn't matter; I still laughed at the way she was drowsy and not completely aware of her actions. She looked right at me with a childish glint in her eyes.

"What are you laughing at, you big oaf?"

"You, you're always finding a way to get into trouble."

"It's not my fault that Jackson went on a murder spree, and I just happened to be the one that almost died." Blake's face was starting to become serious again, which meant the medicine was starting to wear off, and soon, she would be back to the regular Blake who showed no emotion. I should have gotten a picture or video of her like this. Then, as I began to think about everything that I had heard about what had happened ,I wanted to know if maybe she did something to offend the Blue Tiger Gang. But maybe that was a question for another time.

"So, Jackson, you want to tell her what the plan is or shall I?" Jackson looked at me with annoyance.

"Blake, don't freak out, but you and I are going to be staying at Lucian's for a while until things calm down at the house." Jackson said in a timid voice probably hoping that Blake wouldn't get mad at him for making this decision without her. Blake took a deep breath and looked straight in my direction.

"And you agreed to do this?"

"If it keeps you safe, then yes, I will let you stay with me." I could see the surprise in her eyes. I knew she didn't expect me to care, but I didn't expect her to be this surprised that I wasn't a bad guy.

"Jackson! Why didn't you consider that I didn't want to do this?"

"I did, but you were kinda unconscious and in surgery, so I did what I thought was best." Blake was about to say something when the nurse walked in and asked us to leave.

We got into the lobby and sat there for a few minutes, thinking about what to do next. I got up to leave the hospital.

"What are you doing?" Jackson asked.

"We have to go get you and Blake's things that you are going to take. Don't we?" He nodded and got up to leave. We got to the car and took off towards Jackson's house. The entire ride was silent; the only noise was the engine running. We pulled up through the gates and through the long, twisting road up to the house. I had never actually seen the house, but I'm sure if I had, I would remember. The house was huge, granted it was old and probably wouldn't sell for as much as it would've if it was brand new, but it was definitely a work of art. Standing on the porch was a dark-haired woman and a small boy, along with what looked like a maid. Before I could even put the car into park, Jackson was out of the car and walking towards the house. I hopped out of the car and caught up with him. We were walking up the stairs, and I realized that Jackson had a facial expression as if he was going to murder someone.

"Jackson, what are you doing bringing this thing to our home?" The dark-haired woman said, looking me up and down as if I was a rat that was trying to steal food. The look she gave me was of disgust and horror.

"He is one of us, not a monster, Mother, and I am only here to collect Blake's and my clothes."

When he said that, the woman's mouth formed into a very tense frown and her eyes had an angry glaze over them.

"That girl is still alive!" You could hear and see the anger blazing from within. I couldn't stand the thought of Blake having to live with this monster of a woman. Thinking about it was agonizing enough seeing it would kill me from the inside out.

"Just move out of the way; I have neither the time nor the energy to deal with you right now." Jackson went to walk through the door and shoved his shoulder into his mother's as he walked past.

"Your father is leaving, so I guess it will just be me and Philip staying at the house. Well, with Thalia, of course," she said with humor.

"Don't worry. Once Philip is old enough, he will leave, and so will Thalia. Then you can have your evil thoughts to plan out." Jackson walked inside, and I followed. I shut the door when we walked in, so we didn't have to listen to his mother continue her rant about how she was going to fix the family and take Blake out of it. We made our way up the stairs and to Jackson's room. There were blood stains all over the floor. You could tell someone had been scrubbing the floor, trying to get rid of the stains, but they had no such luck.

"Is this where your mother tried to kill Blake?" I could barely say without hinting at disgust.

"I guess. If you think this is bad don't go into the bathroom." There was a sadness to his voice. I knew that he thought that Blake getting hurt was his fault, and that he was responsible for her almost dying.

We finally got all of Blake's and Jackson's belongings out of the house and into the car. We were about to leave when Jackson's mother came running out of the house. She grabbed Jackson by the shoulders.

"Please, Jackson, you can't help this girl. She will only tear the family apart by being the reason you die." I was sitting in the car when she said this and watched as Jackson turned, ignored his mother, and we left.

We got back to the hospital in the middle of the night. We walked into Blake's room, but the only problem was, she wasn't there. Jackson started to freak out. He ran down the hallway, probably trying to find a nurse and ask them were Blake was. I was about to start following him when I heard the bathroom door open. Blake stepped out wearing her clothes that had been washed and her hair was in two braids.

"Did Jackson just run out of the room?" she asked glancing at the door. I started to laugh and nodded towards her. She walked to the door and down the hall following Jackson's footsteps.

I followed her until we got to the counter, where we checked her out of the hospital. Jackson didn't say anything the whole ride; Blake stared out the window, and I drove while listening to the radio.

We finally arrived at my house. It wasn't huge like Jackson's, but it wasn't tiny either. It was a three-bedroom, two-bath with a living room and kitchen. It was white with light blue trim, and the paint was peeling a little, which gave it an older look. I stepped out of the car and heard a girlish yelp!

I turned to look at where it came from just in time to see Jackson fall on the ground laughing. I ran around the car and right as I turned around the back of the car slipped and fell right into the mud with Blake. Blake was laughing and had mud on her face, clothes, and trailed all the way up her arms.

"It's not that funny, Jackson! What if you were the one who fell in the mud? Would it be funny then?" Blake was no longer laughing. She had a grin on her face and was sitting in the mud, waiting for someone to help her up. When Jackson reached to help her up, though, instead of just getting out of the mud, she pulled Jackson down into the mud with us. We all sat there and laughed. I don't know if Blake and Jackson felt the same, but for once I actually felt like a normal teenager.

We rinsed off with the water hose that was beside the house. After we rinsed off, Blake and Jackson grabbed some clothes to change into, and we went inside. I showed them around the kitchen and living room and walked down the hall to where the rooms were.

"This is your room, Blake." I pointed to the room across from mine. She opened the door and looked inside. The room was medium-size and was decorated in black and silver with a hint of green. The bed cover was black with a spotted silver and green design. The walls were a light grey and the floor a black stained wood. Blake walked in and stood looking around. She set her stuff on the bed and took off her shoes. I went to show Jackson his room when Blake called from the doorway of her room.

"Lucian, where is the bathroom?"

"Follow me. It's right by Jackson's room." Jackson's room was on the other side of the house, along with the guest bathroom.

"The bathroom is right there," I said, pointing to the door next to Jackson's room. I opened the door to Jackson's room, which was decorated in red, orange, and brown.

"Sorry about the color I haven't had a chance to remodel it."

"It's fine as long as it has a bed, a roof, and a dresser." Jackson started putting his things away as I turned and started walking to the kitchen. I went straight to my room to go to sleep.

The next morning, I woke up to the smell of eggs and sausage. I went to my bathroom fixed my hair and brushed my teeth. Then went to the kitchen where I found an unusual sight. It was Blake cooking breakfast while listening to music. I sat at the table in the middle of the room and laughed as she tried to flip a pancake into the air and catch it. She finally noticed that I was there and turned off the music.

"What are doing up?"

"I smelt the sausage burning and thought I would come and eat."

"Yeah, well, it's not done yet, and you almost made me drop the pancake," she said as she put the cooked pancake down on a plate.

"Where is Jackson?"

"He's taking a shower." I could see the stitches in her leg and arm when she turned to grab more pancake batter or sausage.

"You can stop staring." I hadn't even realized that I was.

"You should be resting that leg and arm, not cooking breakfast." I stood up and walked over to the counter closest to the where Blake was cooking.

"I'm fine. I have to be ready for anything. People who want to hurt others aren't going to wait for me to rest." I grabbed her shoulder and turned her to look at me. Her eyes were bright green.

"You need to take care of yourself. I couldn't bear to live with myself if something happened to you while you were here." I cupped her face with my hand as I looked into her eyes.

"I'm sorry, am I interrupting something?"

I stepped away from Blake as she turned to look at Jackson. Jackson was standing there looking at us while his hair was dripping wet with water. He looked at me, and I could see the anger and jealousy.

"Lucian, can I talk to you for a minute." Jackson turned and walked down the hall.

"What's up, Jackson?"

"If I knew you were going to be pulling stunts like that, I wouldn't have brought her here."

"I wasn't pulling anything; I genuinely care about Blake." Before he could say anything else Blake called from the kitchen.

"Breakfast is ready." Me and Jackson walked over to the table that everything was at and sat down on either side of Blake.

"You know I could hear everything that y'all were saying, right?" She said as calm as possible. I felt my face go red as I thought about what I said. After she said that, we ate in silence.

After breakfast, we all helped clean up and went to our separate rooms.

Chapter 4

Blake

I walked into my room and threw myself onto my bed. I couldn't stop thinking about what had just happened in the kitchen. How Lucian talked and held me, it was driving me crazy. Even though I could feel the emotion, I had to block it out. I couldn't show Lucian or even Jackson that I had emotions beyond what they had already knew me to have.

I was about to fall asleep when there was a knock at the door.

"Come in." Lucian opened the door and walked in. He was wearing a tux and tie. His jet black hair was slicked back, and he had shades in his hand.

"Hey, I was wondering if maybe you wanted to go to game night with some of the people from school with me?"

"I don't know, Lucian, I almost died yesterday accidentally running into the wrong people at school. Also, I don't have anything nice to wear."

"It's okay, none of the people who attacked you will be there, and I have something for you to wear." He walked over to my closet and pulled a box from the top. He brought the box over to the bed and opened it. Inside the box was a blue and white dress. The dress was white with blue dots and tied around the neck. The dress also had a blue patterned belt. It wasn't really my style, but it was pretty.

"This is gorgeous. Thank you, Lucian." I looked up into his emerald green eyes. He was only a few inches away from me, and all I could think about was what happened in the kitchen.

"I got it yesterday after school as a gift for you." He turned and looked away, breaking eye contact.

"Why would you do that after how I hurt you?"

"Honestly, I don't know. I just have this feeling to take care of you." I could see the red from his face.

"I... I will go with you, but I am not wearing a dress, okay?"

"Okay, that's fine you can wear whatever you like. I will leave you to get ready."

"Thank you, Lucian, for...for everything you have done for me."

"You're welcome, Blake. We are leaving in 20 minutes, and Jackson is coming." He turned towards the door and went to walk out. When he opened the door, Jackson fell on the floor.

"I am going..."

"I already told her that you were going. Also, you might want to eat something before we leave." Lucian laughed as he walked down the hall. Jackson got up off of the floor and looked like a child who got caught stealing candy.

"Were you eavesdropping?"

"What? Of course not." He hurried down the hall. I shut the door hard but not hard enough to slam the door. How dare he eavesdrop on my conversations. He made me so mad. I carefully put the dress back in the box and put it in the top of the closet.

I pulled out a relatively nice black shirt and white pants from my clothes. I threw my hair into a fishtail braid. I looked in the mirror to see how I looked and realized that I had a bruise on the side of my face. I didn't know where it had come from, but I guess it didn't really matter at the moment. I walked out into the hallway where Jackson and Lucian where standing. Both of them were in tuxedos and ties. Lucian was certainly taller than Jackson now that I looked at them both side by side.

"You ready to go?" Jackson asked but didn't look at me.

"No, Jackson, I came out of my room fully dressed to sit on the couch and eat potato chips while y'all go have fun."

Lucian burst out laughing.

"Someone's in the dog house."

We walked to the car, careful not to slip in the mud again.

We drove for three hours. I laid down in the back trying to sleep, but Lucian and Jackson wouldn't stop talking about cars the whole way there. When we finally got there, it was dark. The building had no windows, just a single door. I didn't like the thought of that.

"Are there going to be humans in there?" I said before we got to the door.

"Yes, there are a lot of humans in there along with our kind. Don't worry. You really think me or you're guard dog will let anything happen to you?" He looked at me as he said it, and I could see the affection in his eyes. I could tell he cared about me, but I didn't know why. I felt someone trying to get inside my head as we got closer to the door.

"Jackson, I might need your barrier tonight." Jackson turned to me as I said it. No not to me. There was someone behind me. I turned around as fast as I could, but by the time I turned to look at who was behind me a hand smacked me to the ground. The next thing I saw was a cloth go over my nose. Then blackness.

I woke up in a haze. I was sat upright in a wooden chair tied with a rope. I tried to move my hands, but they were bound by wire and metal cuffs. I looked around but couldn't tell where I was. The room was concrete, had no windows, and a metal door. As far as I could tell, I was the only one in the room. Neither Jackson nor Lucian was with me. I wasn't going to say anything because I wanted as much time to think about how to get out before the people who took me knew I was awake.

I tried to pull my hands through the metal cuffs, but they were too tight. I tried to stand and move my legs, but the rope was wrapped around my legs and the chair. I was about to yell for help when the door opened. I was as calm as I could manage.

"Even after living, you still managed to end up in another life or death situation."

"Who are you?"

"You don't remember." The person stepped into what little light there was. When I saw who it was I couldn't hide my surprise. It was the guy that attacked me in the hallway. I calmed down before he got into my head.

"Why did you kidnap me, and where are Jackson and Lucian?"

"Calm down, Lucian is safely in his car, and Jackson... Well, he can tell you where he is." I was confused when he said that. Then the door opened again and the guy left. A while later, the door opened again. The person who came in the door didn't surprise me at all. It was Julie, Jackson's mom; of course she had something to do with this.

"Hello, Blake. How's your stay been?" She laughed like a crazy person.

"Julie. Why am I not surprised that you did this."

"I only did this because you are tearing my family apart. First you take Jackson, then you make my husband leave me, and now Thalia snuck away. Who's next? Philip? I will not let you tear my family apart any longer!" She walked over and turned on a much brighter light. There was a table underneath the light. The table had surgical tools on it.

"You are going to tell me what my family has been trying to get you to tell us since you were a little girl." So, this wasn't about her family or her pride it was about the same thing her family has been looking for generations.

"I will never tell you where it is, and if you hurt me, Jackson will never forgive you."

"You really think that I care if Jackson forgives, or even loves, me? Right now, Jackson is on the other side of that wall, tied to a chair looking through a one way mirror watching. If you don't tell me what I want to know, Jackson will watch you die."

"How could you do that to your own son!"

"I only had Jackson to continue the bloodline. I don't care what happens to him as long as he doesn't die." She walked over with a hammer and chisel. She put the chisel on my wrist.

Chapter 5

Julie

Does it sound bad if I said that I enjoyed hearing Blake scream? No? It doesn't? Okay. I smashed the hammer down on her wrist again, listening as the bones cracked and splintered. She deserved this. She deserved to be hurting. She ruined my family. I had everything perfect, and then she came along and tore it to shreds. There was blood everywhere from her wrists. My hands stained red, but she didn't break. I couldn't even sense the fear from her. I had to give in to the girl; she had a strong will.

I left the room after an hour of torturing her. She never broke not once. I went to the room that Jackson was being held in.

"I hate you with all that I am!" That's the first thing I heard when I entered the room. It stung, but only for a minute.

"I never said you had to like me. All you had to do was remain loyal to your family and especially me. Instead, you go and betray me for that girl."

"I will always pick Blake over you." There was anger and passion coming from him. The two things I feed off of.

"That's a shame, considering that if she doesn't tell me what I want to know, I will kill her, and once she does tell me, I will kill her anyway." I went towards a sink to wash the blood red stain from my hands. "Your girlfriend does have great self-control though. She hasn't screamed once since I have tortured her." I looked back at Jackson just in time to see the cuffs on his wrists turning green. He was trying to use his ability to open the cuffs. "I wouldn't do that if I were you." I walked over to Jackson and touched his arm, diminishing his powers and growing my own.

"So that's your ability. You take someone else's power and make it your own." He was about to faint.

"Yes, that's my ability, and that's also why no one has ever beat me." I started walking towards the door back to where Blake was. When I reached for the door, I couldn't open it.

"What did you do, Jackson?"

"I made it to where only I or Blake could open that door. No one is getting out of here without me or Blake opening the door, and I also unlocked Blake's cuffs." Jackson smiled as he said it. I walked to the one-way mirror and saw that Blake was now standing in the middle of the room, unravelling the last of the rope.

"Did I forget to mention I also used my mind link to tell Blake what your ability is? Oops."

I could feel the rage coming over of my body. My own son just set me up! Blake started walking to the door that led out of the room. The two Blue Tiger gang members that were in the room pulled the guns from their belts ready to shoot. They both fell over, screaming in agony. The door opened, and Blake entered.

"You know, you should really have told them to not try and get into my head." Blake said, looking at the guards. I slowly tried backing up to get the gun off of the counter behind me.

"You shouldn't do that. I know your ability now and can hurt you really badly if you don't do what I say."

"You can't make me do anything."

She laughed, and then there was a surge of pain that hit me like a wave. My vision went black, and all I could feel was the heat and pressure on my head like a ton of bricks. It felt like someone was burning me from the inside out.

"Okay… Okay. I will do what you say." The pain died, and I could see a little.

"Undo Jackson's cuffs. Now!"

I slowly moved towards the chair and undid the cuffs. Blake moved towards Jackson and lifted him with his arm around her shoulders. There was still blood dripping from her hands and wrists.

"Now, stay there, and be a good little puppet." She smiled, walked out the door and closed it.

I was stuck in the room with two dead Blue Tiger gang members until I could figure a way out. And once I got out, I was going to kill Blake Laurels.

Chapter 6

Lucian

I woke up in my car in the parking lot. There was blood coming out of my nose. I heard tapping on the window. It was a girl; not just any girl, it was the maid from Jackson's house. I slowly got out of the car.

"Are you okay?"

"Yes, I'm fine." I was trying to think back and remember what happened, but the only thing I could remember was Julie, Jackson's mom. I didn't trust the girl who just woke me up, she was working for Julie last time I saw her. I walked up to the girl, and every time I stepped forward, she stepped back. I pushed her against the wall holding her wrists with my hands.

"Where are they? Where are Blake and Jackson? I know you are working for Julie!"

"I don't know where they are; I ran away from Julie two days ago." I knew she was telling the truth because of the fear in her eyes. We stood there for a few minutes, looking into each other's eyes. There was something special about her. Her eyes were a blueish-green and held so much emotion in them. She was short. Shorter than Blake. The way she held herself made her look like an innocent child who didn't know what was going on. Her hair shown in the sunlight, changing between white and gold.

"Uhh... Can you let me go?" I backed away slowly, taking in every detail of her face one last time.

"What's your name?" I asked, remembering that I didn't know her name, only that she was a maid.

"Thalia." She rubbed her wrists that were red.

"Well, Thalia, could you help me find Blake and Jackson?"

"Sure, but you have to promise not to do that again." She was still rubbing her wrist.

"Sorry." I genuinely felt bad. We went to a restaurant first because Thalia wanted food, and I needed to feed off of someone. We walked in and sat down at a table. While Thalia ordered I walked around and syphoned off of people who were hungry. By the time I sat back down at the table, the food was already there. Thalia had gotten herself a BLT and ordered me a breakfast plate. Even though I felt I knew I had to eat actual food to get my strength back, I could go a month without human food but only about a week before I needed to syphon emotions.

"So, where do you think Julie took Blake and Jackson?" Thalia said biting into her BLT.

"I don't really have any idea. The only thing I know is that she was working with the Blue Tiger Gang. She had to of taken them back to one of the hideouts or warehouses the Blue Tiger Gang owns." I knew of one nearby, but just because it was nearby didn't mean that it was the one they were at. There could be hundreds in the state that they could be at. I didn't know what to do.

"You could just have the police put out a search party for them."

"The police have never been able to do anything for our kind."

"Well, have you ever given them a chance?"

"No, and I don't plan to start today."

I put the money down on the table and started to walk out of the restaurant. I could hear Thalia get up and follow me. I got into the car and waited for her to get in before starting it.

"Where are we going?" She didn't shut the door until I told her:

"I know someone who's good at tracking people down. We are going to meet him."

Thalia shut the door and buckled up.

When we got to the park where we were meeting him at it was nearly dark and there were very few people around. He was standing next to the pond, watching the ducks fighting over some bread.

"Hi, Lucian. Who did you bring with you?" He said without turning around.

"No one of your concern. I just need your help; I don't want any trouble." This time, he turned around to look at me and Thalia.

"Who are you trying to find now?" He walked over to a bench and sat down while me and Thalia stood.

"I need help finding two of my friends who were taken by the Blue Tiger Gang."

"I will help, but only for a price," he said while looking at Thalia. He fed off of the emotion of selfishness. I knew he would want to feed, and I didn't think to tell Thalia. When she noticed what was happening, she started to back up slowly. I turned and grabbed her arm, walking her a few feet away.

"Look, I know you didn't sign up for this and that you don't want to do this, but he doesn't feed off good emotion he feeds off of selfishness. It's not going to change how you act or how you feel. He is only taking away something bad, I promise." She stood there for a few minutes, looking at me with her greyish blue eyes. I almost told her she couldn't do it just because I couldn't stand anyone even touching her for some reason.

"Okay, I will do it, but only because this is the quickest way to get to Blake and Jackson." We walked back over to where the guy was sitting on the bench.

"Are you ready to find where your friends are?" The guy got up and touched my arm. He needed a memory of Blake and Jackson in order to track them to where they were.

"Okay, I am seeing through the girl's eyes. The guy is passed out in her arms. It looks like they are walking along a highway in the country. The girl is… wait she's talking to me while I'm in her head? She said to tell you that they are heading to the house. It looks like her wrists are broken!" He stumbled backwards holding his head in pain.

"She blocked me out of her head. How did she do that, Lucian? I won't take any payment I just want to know how she did that." He looked curious as if he was truly concerned, but why would he be concerned?

"Why do you want to know how she does that?"

"So I can know the extent of her abilities."

"She is human. she doesn't have abilities. She uses her mental will to block us out."

He pulled out a phone and started dialing a number that I didn't recognize. I turned back to look at Thalia and looked at the car that was at least 100 feet away. I looked back at the guy that was now talking on the phone and pacing back and forth. I walked toward the guy and touched his arm. He had no idea what my abilities were, so I had the advantage, but only for a few minutes.

"You are in love with that woman walking over there and will do anything to be with her." The guy took off running towards the lady, and of course, she ran away from him.

I grabbed Thalia's arm and pulled her with me as I ran towards the car.

"What's wrong?" she asked while she buckled her seatbelt.

"That guy was going to sell us out to someone and take Blake, so they could figure out how her mind works and how to stop it. My kind don't like humans who can fight back. Especially not hunters who can fight back." I started toward my house, knowing that that was where Blake was going.

"What do you mean hunters?"

I rolled my eyes. Humans know nothing; she had spent years with that family and still knew nothing.

"Blake is a hunter of my kind. They call us Shaitans, which means related to an evil spirit or the devil. The hunters hunt our kind and choose which of us are good enough to stay on Earth. I have never heard of a hunter who could block us out of their minds before though."

We were driving down a highway in the middle of nowhere when we saw Blake and Jackson on the side of the road. Jackson was on the ground passed out, and Blake was waving us down. I put my car in park and ran to see if they were okay.

"What happened? Are you okay?" I grabbed Blake by the shoulders and checked if shehad any cuts or bruises. Her wrists had dry blood running down them and were in bad shape. It looked like a dog had been mauling on them all day as if they were a bone. I wrapped my arms around her, and for once she showed emotion. She hugged me back and nearly fell to the ground. I could feel her pain and fear.

"It's okay. Everything's okay. Go get in the car, and I will get Jackson, then we can go home, I promise." She walked over to the car and got into the back on the driver side. I lifted Jackson into the passenger side.

When we got to the house, I first got out and carried Jackson inside to his room, so he could sleep. Then I had to carry Thalia (who had fallen asleep on the way) inside to the couch. Bb the time I had gotten to Blake, she was already awake and out of the car.

"I think I am going to go take a shower and go to bed," she said as she walked passed me.

"Okay." I cleaned the blood stains off the seats in the car and turned it off. When I got inside, I realized Thalia wasn't on the couch anymore and walked around the house checking rooms. I finally checked Blake's room, and there she was passed out in Blake's bed. The only problem was, where was Blake? She wasn't in Jackson's room or on the couch. The only other room was mine but, there was no way she would sleep in my room.

I opened the door and turned on the light.

"Hey! Turn off the damn light some of us like to sleep." Blake was lying in my bed wrapped in a burrito of blankets.

"Why are you in my bed?" I walked to the other side and got into bed.

"My bed was occupied, and I didn't want to wake up our guest. Why? Is there a problem with me sleeping in your bed?"

"No. I am just surprised that's all. I want you to know that I will not be sleeping on the couch." I reached over and turned off the light.

"I know; it's fine. I'm comfortable enough with you." She rolled over and fell asleep. Before I knew it, I was deep in sleep.

I got woken up with cold water. Jackson was standing at the foot of my bed. Blake had sometime throughout the night moved to where she was right by my side, woken up by the same cold water. Jackson must have thrown it on us.

"What the hell, Jackson!" Blake was pissed, and frankly, so was I. Jackson threw the bowl that had the water down on the bed.

"I wake up in bed at Lucian's house after remembering that we were being tortured and come to find you in bed with Lucian cuddled up like a happy couple. What am I supposed to do!"

Blake had gotten out of bed and was putting MY robe on.

"I don't know. You could just leave us alone and wait till we get up to ask us what had happened while you were knocked out!" Blake was now yelling at Jackson, who looked hurt by the fact that she was mad at him.

"Are you just going to sit there or are you going to say something?" Jackson was now looking at me.

"What do you want me to say, Jackson? I was knocked out when they took y'all. I didn't know what was happening and then I ran into your nanny, who, when we got home, took Blake's room. Blake came here out of her own free will. I didn't mind control her; I didn't seduce her. I am just as pissed as she is!"

Thalia walked into the room and looked at all three of us. Her hair was sticking up in five different ways.

"Okay! One, can y'all stop yelling? Two, I am not a nanny, and three, I didn't know that was Blake's room."

All at once they all three started yelling at each other about different things when a gunshot ran through the house. They all stopped yelling, and I told them to get down. I pressed my index finger to my lips telling them to be quiet and went to the windows. What I saw outside the window made me even more mad than when Jackson poured water on me and Blake. I turned and looked at Thalia.

"That guy that we met with called us in."

Outside, there were over 10 cars full of Shaitans.

"Is there a back door?" Thalia asked. I could feel the fear coming from her. I shook my head and went over to my closet. As I moved the boxes on the bottom of my closet Blake, Jackson and Thalia all crowded around me. I opened a latch in the bottom of my closet. I let Blake go first since they wanted her. Then it was Thalia and Jackson. It was finally my turn to go down, and I could hear the strangers burst through the door. I got a look at who it was that was looking for us right as I closed the door. The tunnel was lit with forensic lights on both sides. Blake had her arms wrapped around her waist, clenching onto the robe, and even though her body language showed fear, her face was calm and content. Jackson was holding Thalia in his arms to keep her from shaking.

"Someone want to explain why those people are looking for us, how they found us, and why is there a goddamn tunnel under your house," Blake said, counting them out on her fingers and looking at me.

"We had to ask a guy Lucian knows to help track y'all. Well when you pushed him out of your head, he got excited and called someone. I guess he called some of his friends, and they are looking for you," Thalia answered, still cradled in Jackson's arms. Blake kept a straight face while listening.

"I'm sorry, guys, this is my fault. I shouldn't have showed my powers to that guy." Blake's eyes were on the floor. She couldn't look us in the eye.

I couldn't help but feel bad. This wasn't her fault none of this was her fault. She didn't ask to go through the things she went through when she was little, and she certainly didn't ask for the power she has. Before I realized what I was doing, I was across the tunnel with my hand under her chin, lifting her head to look at me.

"None of us blame you for this, Blake. All of us have contributed to the situation we are in." Her eyes were wet with tears when she buried her face into my chest. I could feel her hand grip my shirt as she held herself together. We all stayed there, trying to gather ourselves and get back to reality.

"So, what are we going to do now?" Thalia was sitting by the wall her head propped up by her elbows.

"I guess we can use the safe house I have down here, and we can go up if we need anything. Those guys are working with the Blue Tiger Gang, so they will be looking for us. We can't go back to school; that's the first place they'll look."

They followed me down the tunnel to the safe house that I had. I built it when I first bought the house, just in case of emergencies.

"There is a small problem with the safe house."

"Great, what's the problem?" Blake said, walking right behind me.

"There are only two bedrooms."

Everyone stopped and looked at each other. I turned and unlocked the door that was right behind me. The safe house looked exactly like my house that we just left; the only difference was that there were no windows. They followed me into the house and looked around. Everything was the same, but there was one less room.

Chapter 7

Blake

"So what are we going to do about the sleeping situation?" I was staring right at Lucian when I asked, but Jackson was the first one to say something.

"I will sleep on the couch, and you girls can take one of the bedrooms, unless of course one of you wants to go sleep in Lucian's room, then Thalia can just have the bedroom to herself."

Jackson didn't look at me when he said that. Was he seriously mad about that?

"It was one time, Jackson; it didn't mean what you think it did." I stared at him, but he never looked up. He just ignored me. "Fine, whatever. You want to be upset about it, then I will sleep in Lucian's room. Maybe I will give you something to be upset about." I couldn't believe that he would say something like that. He finally looked at me, and I saw the hurt in his eyes.

"Okay now that that is settled, I want you to know that we have enough food and supplies, but there is also only one bathroom so whoever wants to take a shower first can go." Lucian was sitting on the couch watching us argue.

After we had decided that Thalia could shower first, we went to get settled in. I followed Lucian to the room we were staying in. I really needed to get something to change into. I was still in my PJs. The room was in the exact same spot as it was in the actual house, but the decoration of it was different. The room was red, blue, and yellow. Maybe to lighten it up because there were no windows.

"Blake, if you don't want to sleep in here you can go to the other room. I'm not going to hold it against you." He was digging through the dresser, probably looking for clothes to change into, but when he found some, he threw them at me instead.

"You can change. I'll go talk to Jackson and try to get him to calm down." He started to leave but turned around when he was in the doorway. "And Blake, don't take this the wrong way because I do really like you, but I will not be used as an object to get back at anyone—especially not Jackson." He closed the door.

While I was changing, I couldn't help but think of what Lucian said. Was I just using him to get back at Jackson, or was it something more? I didn't want to believe that it was either; I think I just trusted him more than Thalia. The shirt he gave me was really baggy, but then again, he was much taller than me. The shorts weren't perfect, but they didn't fall, which is what mattered. Lucian was waiting in the hall when I opened the door. He looked me up and down.

"Is something wrong?"

He looked away when I said that; there was red on his cheeks.

"No, it's just that you look really...uhhh, cute in baggy clothes."

I looked down at the floor trying to keep my composure.

"Thanks I guess." I walked down the hall to the kitchen to look for food. Jackson was in the kitchen making fried eggs and toast. I looked at the food, asking myself whether or not I should ask for some. Jackson turned and looked at me and quickly turned back to the food.

"Would you like some?" he asked, looking down at the food.

"Yes, please that would be great."

"Where's Thalia?"

"She's in her room changing, I guess, but I don't think that there are any girl clothes here. If there were then you wouldn't be in Lucian's clothes cor-rect?" There it was again, that tone of voice that he kept using when he talked about me and Lucian.

"Is there something wrong? Are you jealous that I am sleeping in Lucian's room and not on the couch with you?"

He jumped, throwing his hands in the air. His face was bright red and he wasn't looking me in the eye.

"Wh...Why would you say something like that?" He's a bad liar.

"No reason, just wanted to get a reaction that wasn't aggressive." I was laughing. After we finished eating, I decided to go and talk to Thalia. She still hadn't come out of her room. I knocked on the door.

"Thalia, is everything okay in there?" I tried opening the door, but it was locked.

"Yeah, I… Just hang on a minute." She opened the door letting me inside. She had on a t-shirt that went down to her knees and her pants that she had been wearing the day before. There was something else that bothered me though. She looked nervous, like she was hiding something. Before I knew it, I was pushing her again the way holding her arms behind her back.

"What are you hiding?"

She screamed in agony. The boys came barging in the door, confused as to what was happening.

"What's going on in here?" Jackson tried pulling me off of her, but got a chest full of my elbow instead. He landed on the floor by the bed. Lucian walked beside me where I could see him.

"Blake, let her go or I will use my abilities on you. I don't want to do this."

"Go ahead. I can fend you off."

"Okay then. I am apologizing ahead of time for this." I felt Lucian reach into my mind. It felt like he was pulling me away from reality, like he was trying to make me go into a dream.

When I finally got him out of my head, I was in the hallway leaning against the wall. He must have pulled me away physically while I was trying to fight him mentally.

"I'm sorry, Blake, I didn't want to do that, but you weren't going to let her go if I hadn't of done that she wo…" I pushed him into the wall.

"You know there is such a thing as talking to someone when they are mad. You don't have to jump into their head." I was inches away from him. I couldn't hold it in anymore the anger and sadness overwhelmed me. At some point, I ended up on the floor.

"Blake? Blake, are you okay? Did I hurt you when I went inside your head?" Lucian was right in front of me, holding onto my shoulders.

"Yeah, I'm fine. Just a little tired, that's all." My vision was a little blurry.

"Okay, well, let's get you back to the room, so you can rest. It's been a long day." He lifted me up into his arms, carrying me through the hallway back to the room.

"You know I have my own set of legs, right? I can walk by myself."

"Yeah, I know, but I just didn't want you to take off back to Thalia's room." He put me down when we got to the door. I sat down on the bed thinking of what Thalia was trying to hide.

"Lucian, why did y'all pull me away from her? You know she's hiding something." He didn't look at me he just sat down beside me.

"I know she has been hiding something from the first day we met her, but I didn't want to scare her and tackle the information out of her." He had a point; I shouldn't have reacted the way I did.

"I'm sorry I overreacted."

He finally looked at me, and I was surprised to see amusement.

"I'm not the one who you have to apologize to. I don't think you did anything wrong, but Jackson, on the other hand, thinks you tried to kill her." He stood up and walked to the door. "Try to get some sleep, okay?" He went to leave but the door wouldn't open.

"What the hell? Jackson! What did you do to the door?" Lucian was banging on the door, trying to get out. I stood up. Why would Jackson do this?

"I'm sorry, I can't let you out; not if it means Blake gets out. I can't let her hurt Thalia again." He sounded like a robot, like he was being manipulated.

"I won't try to leave I promise, just let him out!" It was a lie, of course; I would try to leave. Something wasn't right.

"No, she told me not to let you out, so I can't let you out." I stepped back nearly tripping over something on the floor.

"Lucian, something's wrong. I have a bad feeling."

"So do I." Lucian tried everything to get out of the room; he tried to break the door, take the hinges out, and even go through the walls. Nothing worked. It was like we were in a box only Jackson could open.

"Let me try. Maybe I can break through the spell." I got up and touched the door handle. I felt the energy run through my fingers as my mind tried to figure out what kind of spell he used. As soon as I started to unravel the spell, it threw my power right back at me. I went flying across the room, hitting the wall.

"Blake! Are you okay?" Lucian was by my side, sitting me up.

"Yes. I found out what kind of spell he used. We can't open the door unless Thalia says, so it's a command spell."

"Great what now?"

I looked at him and for the first time felt fear coming off of him.

"I don't know."

We sat in the room for what seemed like forever. Every day, it was the same routine we would get toast for breakfast, lunch, and dinner. We never got let out to take a shower; the only time we got to use the bathroom was when we were both handcuffed. Every day, we would sit there and talk until Jackson came to get us. It was torture. Jackson didn't talk to us or help us. He didn't even have emotion in his eyes. Lucian couldn't use his abilities because he didn't have enough energy, and I couldn't use mine because anytime I did, it was like someone throwing me through a wall.

"Get up, Blake." Thalia came in the room and put the cuffs on Lucian but instead of doing the same for me she cuffed me to the dresser. Jackson came in after her, looking as emotionless as always. He walked over to me.

"Julie wants some info about the thing you know about. So, I'm going to leave you here with my good friend Jackson until you tell us what we want to know."

I spat at her and said some insults that I didn't regret.

"Have fun, and Jackson, don't by any means stop until she says she'll talk, okay?"

Jackson nodded, and Thalia left to do whatever she was doing while we had been in this room.

"Tell us what we want to know, and I won't hurt you too much."

I looked him in the eye and saw no trace of the friend I once had.

"Never!"

Jackson reared back and kicked me in the side. I heard a snap and crack of my bones.

"Answer the question." Jackson's face remained emotionless. I don't understand why, or even how, Thalia got him to be like this.

"N...No" He stood on my ankle, putting all his weight on it while he stomped on my knee, sending pain throughout my leg.

The torture and pain went on for hours. Every time I would deny him the information, he would either kick me or stomp on one of my limbs. Sometimes he pulled me off the ground from my hair. If Lucian was saying something, I couldn't hear him. I had blacked out from the pain. I woke up in the bed untied. Lucian was by my side.

"Blake?" He leaned over and brushed the strands of hair out of my face.

"What happened?"

He looked away from me towards the door.

"After you blacked out, Jackson left. I finally got the handcuffs off and untied you, but you have three broken ribs, a broken ankle, and a bruise on your face." His hand was clenching the blanket from the anger. "I swear, I will kill him if we can't get him back to normal, and I am going to kill Thalia no matter what."

I grabbed his hand.

"We have to get out of here, Lucian, before they kill one of us."

"We can't leave until your foot heals." He bent over and uncovered my foot. The foot was purple and black.

"That's going to take at least three more weeks. We won't make it that long." I looked at him. "We have to get out of here."

"I'll give you my food for five days, so you can have your abilities back. That's the only way we are going to get out of here."

"Okay," Lucian agreed.

We laid there until our food got there. Lucian got up to get the two pieces of bread.

"At least eat for today." Lucian handed me the piece of bread. I guessed it wouldn't hurt to eat today. After we ate, I tried getting up.

"What are you doing?" Lucian looked at me confused.

"I need to change. There is blood all over these clothes."

Lucian's face got red, and he looked away.

"I won't be able to leave."

"Umm… Lucian I can't walk, so you have to get the clothes, and you can just look away."

He got up and looked through the drawers. He pulled out pajama shorts and a long formal shirt. After he gave them to me, he turned toward a corner. I tried on the shorts and shirt. The shorts were way too big, but the shirt fit fine.

"Uhh, so, the shorts didn't really fit." Lucian turned around his face flustered.

"I don't have any other bottoms that could fit, I'm sorry." He walked over and sat down.

"It's okay." I climbed into the bed. Lucian laid down right next to me.

"What happens if we don't get out of here, Blake?" Lucian was looking into my eyes. I could see the calmness as well as the fear. I reached out and put my hand on his cheek.

"At least I will spend my time with someone I care about then."

Before I could stop myself, I was kissing Lucian. I didn't want to die and leave everything I felt under the table. It felt nice to feel like someone cared about me. I ran my hands through his hair, which was softer and longer than it should have been. When we pulled away, I looked into his green eyes. We laid there together until the lights went out. I didn't want to leave his side, not at the moment. I fell asleep on his chest, listening to his heart beat.

The morning came without warning. I woke up to someone yanking me out of bed my hair.

"Let go!" I clawed at the person's arm. They let go with a shout of pain. It was Thalia.

"You stupid girl!" There was blood running down her arm. I looked around, searching for Lucian. He was being held back by four guys. They had him gagged with a rag. He looked at me with fear and anger. I turned back to look at Thalia. The door was wide open. I stood with all my weight on my ankle. When Thalia went to grab me, I threw all my weight into her, knocking her off balance. Jackson came running into the room at the same time two of the men holding Lucian let go of him to come restrain me. Jackson pulled me off of Thalia just as Lucian punched him in the side of the face. Lucian grabbed my arm and pulled me through the door, closing it on the other side.

"Are you okay?"

"Yeah, but we need to get out of here before they open the door."

When we got out of the house and made our way through the tunnel and up the ladder, we looked for any signs of people.

"Do you have the keys to your car?" He went to his dresser and pulled a spare set of keys out of the top drawer.

"Got them, do you want to grab clothes? I have to grab cash then we will leave."

I grabbed my bag that I kept under my bed. It had all of my clothes and money not used when I was on my own. I met Lucian out in the car. We drove as far as we could as fast as we could.

"What are we going to do now?" I looked at Lucian.

"I guess we'll find somewhere to stay until we can get Jackson back to himself." I didn't know what they did to Jackson; I didn't even know if we could change him back to how he was.

I woke up, and we were at a hotel. The red light of the sign shown through the car window. Jackson wasn't in the car. I couldn't get out of the car because of my ankle. I decided to just sit and wait; not like I had any choice anyway. I dozed in and out of sleep when Lucian finally came back to the car.

"Sorry, I had to make some calls and check us in. We are booked for a week and then one of my good friends is coming to take us to one of their holiday homes here." He pushed his head against the steering wheel probably exhausted from the drive.

"Do you want to go inside and get settled in?"

"Yeah, that sounds like a good idea. A shower also sounds great."

We finally got inside and locked the doors. We made sure to close all the curtains; we couldn't risk Thalia and them finding us, not after we just got out of that place. I threw my bag into the closet, not wanting to unpack in case we had to leave quickly.

"You can shower first, and I will turn on the AC." The AC sounded great right now.

I gathered my clothes and limped my way to the bathroom. Instead of taking a shower, which involved standing, I took a bath. I was so grateful I packed razors when I packed my bag. It felt so nice to wear shorts and a shirt that fit me without having to worry about my legs being hairy. The hotel room was nice enough to where it didn't look like a dump.

The room was freezing by the time I came out of the out of the bathroom.

"Is it too cold?" Lucian walked over to me and put his hand on my cheek. His hand was warm against my skin.

"No, it should be fine when we get under the blankets." I put my hand over his. My hand was much smaller than his, but they fit together perfectly.

"I should probably go take a shower now."

"Okay, I'm going to lay down."

He went to the bathroom. I laid down in the bed. The mattress wasn't horrible. The blanket was comfortable and warm. I sat at the end of the bed. I couldn't believe what happened; I would have never thought that Thalia would be working for Julie, especially not after that night when I helped her. I didn't even know what she did to Jackson.

"Hey, are you alright? You look kinda sad."

"Yeah, I'm just thinking about everything." Lucian sat on the opposite side of the bed.

"I know what you mean. I can't stop thinking of how we are going to get Jackson back." We slid under the blankets. Lucian wrapped his arms around my waist pulling me in. I felt safe in his arms. It felt right, but at the same time, there was a bad feeling about it.

"Goodnight, Blake." He kissed the side of my cheek sending goosebumps down my arms.

"Goodnight, Lucian." I reached over and turned off the lamp that was next to the bed and laid my hand on top of Lucian's.

Waking up the next morning wasn't in pain or in screaming or any horrible way. I woke up with the sun peeking through the curtains and Lucian holding me. It honestly felt like a dream, but when I tried to move my ankle and pain struck, I remembered that it was reality. I turned to where I could see Lucian. He was still passed out. My arm wrapped around his neck, and I was running my fingers through his black hair when his eyes fluttered open.

"Good morning, beautiful." He leaned over and gave me a soft kiss on the lips.

"Did you sleep well?"

"Yes, better than I have in a while." It was nice to see him smile.

"Can we just lay here for bit?" I didn't want to get up and go back into reality. I wanted to lay here and be with him until we could no longer sit here and had to get up for water.

"Of course we can." We laid there talking and laughing just being in the moment. Every once in a while we would kiss, but other than that, it was just us talking. It was noon by the time we got out of bed.

"Do you want to get room service and then we can go and take you to get something for your ankle?" He started to get up and putting his shoes on.

"Yeah, we can order food, but if you're going somewhere, we need to stick together, okay?" He nodded his head. I called room service and asked for some waffles with eggs and sausage. It smelled so good when it got here that I forgot that one of the plates was Lucian's and almost ate it. After we ate, I put my bag in the backseat of the car, and we went to the store. We had to get an ankle brace to help with my foot. We also grabbed some pain killers for the swelling. When we got back to the car, I had to put my foot in the middle seat, so Lucian could help me put it on.

"Okay, so what now?" He looked at me

"I guess we need to find Jackson's dad to find some answers."

"How do we do that? Julie said that he left her."

"We can go to their house and see if he came back. If not, then we will figure it out." I guess I looked hopeless or upset because Lucian reached over and grabbed my hand.

"It going to be okay. We'll figure this out, I promise, we'll get Jackson back." I knew he couldn't keep that promise, but at least one of us had hope.

We stopped at the edge of the trees by Jackson's house. I saw Jackson, his mom, and Thalia sitting on the porch, talking. Well, Julie was more yelling than talking, but I didn't see Jackson's dad.

"He's not here. We need to get out of here before they see us."

"Wait, we don't know if he's inside or not." I grabbed Lucian's arm before he could turn away.

"Well, we can't just walk in the front door and yell his name out to see if he will answer." He was looking towards me for the answer.

"I know, but we can wait until nightfall or until they leave, can't we?"

"I don't know if that's the best idea, given our current condition." He looked down at my ankle, and I realized that he meant me. He didn't think it was a good idea because he didn't think I could handle it.

"I'm fine, okay? If you can handle it, so can I."

"I didn't mean it like that. I know you can handle more than a lot of girls and guys your age and older. I was just saying that you should rest a little more before you charge in there. We don't even know how many people are in there, let alone what abilities they may have."

I knew he just wanted to look after me and not see me get hurt, but I didn't need him to see me as helpless.

"I don't need you to try and protect me and treat me like I'm helpless." I turned to look at the house where Jackson, Thalia, and Julie were all standing. I couldn't believe that his own mother would make him do that. She would turn her own son into a walking zombie with no emotions. My eyes started tearing up. Jackson was the first friend I'd ever had.

We sat there for hour after hour, waiting for them to leave, but they just stood there as if waiting for someone. About five hours later, they finally left to go somewhere. Where they went, I have no idea.

Lucian fell asleep a few feet away, lying on a log. I should have probably woke him up, but he needed his rest. I'd go by myself; it would be quicker anyway. I started making my way to the house, trying not to worry about Lucian waking up or Julie coming back. The stairs creaked as I walked up them, but there was no way to stop them from doing that. The house was old and was going to creak.

"Hello? Is someone here?" I could tell it was Casey's voice from outside.

"Casey, it's me, Blake. Is it okay for me to come inside?" There was a long pause before he answered again.

"I think so, I am in the kitchen—tied to one of the chairs!" I tested the door handle before going inside. Once I was inside, I rushed to the kitchen nearly falling in the process. Casey was tied to one of the dining room chairs, his face was bruised like someone had been hitting him all week. I untied him and let him get comfortable before asking any questions.

"Why did you come back?"

"Because Blake, she's my wife, and they're my children. I can't just up and leave them. I love them."

"I thought you didn't agree with Julie's methods?"

"I don't, but it doesn't change the fact that I will do anything for her, and I will especially put up with her to save my children from her ways." That confused me. I thought he knew what happened with Jackson, but maybe I was wrong.

"Haven't you seen what she's done to Jackson?"

"No! I haven't seen Jackson since I left. Honestly, I haven't seen either of them. Why what did she do?"

"I don't know exactly what she did; all I know is that he acts like an emotionless zombie that follows her every order, and Thalia is in on it, too."

"So, she black minded him?" She what! What is black minded?

"What do you mean black minded?"

"It's one of her abilities. She can take control of someone's mind and black out their emotions and choices. So, I recommend that you don't leave anyone you care about alone." Casey's voice started changing, and then he started laughing before he pulled out a gun from behind his back and pointed it right at my head. I leapt out of the way, and the bullet barely missed me. I took off through the house.

Chapter 8

Lucian

I woke up to the sound of a gunshot. I fell off the log and landed right on a rock. "Okay, well, there goes my stomach." I got off the ground and looked around and then realization hit my right in the gut. I didn't see Blake. I kept saying to myself that she wasn't dumb enough to go into the house by herself. She wouldn't do that, right? Not after I specifically told her not to...

I ran to the edge of the cliff and saw that the screen door of the house was wide open.

"Uggghhh... Why can't she just listen for once? Why does she have to be so freakin' stubborn?"

I ran down the hill and flew into the house. Another gunshot fired somewhere upstairs.

"If you hurt Blake, I will make your life a living hell!"

"My life is already a living hell." Casey? Why was he on Julie's side? Blake told me that he ran away and would only come back to help his kids. I made my way up the stairs.

"Why are you doing this, Casey? Why are you helping Julie? What has she ever done for you?"

"A lot more than this little girl has, and I don't have a choice; I'm doing this for Jackson and Philip."

Now I understood. Julie must have told him if he killed Blake, she would let Jackson and Philip go with him.

"You don't have to do this. We can find another way." I rounded another corner, looking for Blake or even Casey.

"Yes, I do!" I turned around to see him pointing the gun at me this time. Before he could shoot, I knocked the gun out of his hand and grabbed him by the arm. I felt my power surge through me.

"You hate Julie and want nothing to do with her. You love all your kids, even Blake, the girl you adopted. You wouldn't want to do anything to hurt them." I felt him relax and saw the calmness in his eyes. Thank God that worked!

"I'm sorry, Lucian, I never want to hurt Blake. I just want Jackson back."

"I know. We all want him back." I walked down a few more hallways and searched for Blake before nearly walking into her. I was so angry she left without me, but at the same time, I was so happy she wasn't hurt. I don't know what I would've done if she got hurt. I wrapped my arms around her. Then I pulled away.

"What the hell were you thinking, leaving without telling me?" I looked into her eyes and saw tears. I couldn't help but take her in my arms and hold her for a few minutes.

"I'm sorry, but we need to leave before they get back."

"Yeah, of course, let's go." I grabbed her hand and told Casey to follow us, and we left the house, going back to the car. Once we were in the car and leaving, Blake passed out in the passenger seat, and Casey just sat in the back.

We got back to the hotel around midnight. Casey walked up into the room while I carried Blake into the room and laid her down on the bed. Casey slept on the couch that folded out into a bed. I climbed into bed, careful not to wake up Blake, wrapped my arms around her pulling her close to me, and went to sleep.

The morning came as fast as a blink. I woke up, and Blake was lying on my chest, sleeping soundly. Casey was sitting on the couch, watching the TV. I rolled over onto my side, letting Blake's head fall onto my arm. She groaned and slowly opened her eyes.

"Morning, beautiful." She stretched her arms up and around my neck.

"Good morning." She leaned forward and pressed a small kiss to my lips, sending shivers down my back.

"Did you sleep well?" She looked at me with those vibrant green eyes that always draw me to her like a moth to the light.

"Of course I did; I had you beside me." She snuggled up against my chest. I couldn't help but smile at her. "Can we just lay here all day?" She looked up at me.

I wish I could have told her yes, but I knew we had to finish what we started and get Jackson back. As much as I loved the thought of having her to myself and running away with her, I knew that she would never forgive herself if we just left Jackson with Julie.

"I'm afraid not. We have to ask Casey about how we can get Jackson back to normal."

"I know, but it was worth a try." She threw off the blanket and went to the bathroom. It was about 30 minutes before she came back out. Her hair was wet, and she was wearing new clothes.

"Can we go get breakfast please?" She walked behind me and hugged me, but at the same time, grabbed the keys from the table in front of me. Me and Casey followed her out the door. We drove down to a diner that was a few blocks away. Once we ordered and got our drinks, we finally got to the questions.

"So, how do we turn him back to normal?" Blake asked Casey

"Honestly there is only one way to stop her abilities." I knew what he was about to say, but it still shocked me that he hated her that much.

"We have to kill her don't we?" He nodded his head, answering her question. The waiter delivered our food and left. "Okay, so how do we get close enough to do that?" she said after taking a bite of her pancakes.

"Julie is having a ball to celebrate Jackson's return as well as the 300 hundredth year her family has been here. We can go to it and kill her there."

"How will we get inside?"

"There normally aren't guards of any kind at the house because we all have abilities, so it will be easy to slip by."

"And you're sure that Jackson will change back to normal as soon as she's dead?"

"Yes, absolutely sure." We paid the check and left, going back to the hotel. Once inside, we all sat in the living room.

"What happens when Jackson inevitably tries to save her?" We all looked at each other, then me and Casey turned to look at Blake at the same time.

"No! That's a horrible idea. Remember what happened the last time he saw me?" She started to stand up, but I put my hand on her shoulder.

"Calm down you have the power to stop him should he try anything. He cares about you, even if he's mad because of us." She sat back down slowly looking at me with fear in her eyes.

"I'm not scared he'll be mad at us; I'm scared he'll be pissed because I have information that he wants."

Chapter 9

Blake

"Oh, you mean about the cure for our kind?" Casey blurted out, knowing that Lucian didn't know. I glared over at him, trying to make it hurt. Lucian looked back and forth between me and Casey.

"Wait, do you mean to tell me that there is a cure for my kind that can make us normal, and you are the one keeping it from us?"

"Lucian, it's not what y…"

"No, Blake, you have no right to keep that from me and my kind, you have no idea what it's like to be one of us, so why should you be the one that keeps it from us?" I could see the anger and hurt in his eyes a mile away. Given everything that's happened between us, it was hard not to bend underneath the need to make him feel better.

"Look, the cure isn't what you want it to be, and I'm sorry I didn't tell you sooner." He still wouldn't look at me, and it hurt that he wouldn't, but I had to move on to the plan.

"So, how do we keep them from knowing it's us?" Lucian looked at Casey, and he looked at me.

"Simple, Lucian can glamor your mind waves around everyone, and I don't think that Jackson and Julie will be looking for you; so as long as you don't make a scene, we should be fine."

"Okay, so now what do? We wear all are clothes that were left back at Lucian's house?" Lucian finally looked at me.

"I guess we'll just go get them. What's the worst that can happen?" Lucian said in his smug voice, squinting at me.

After we finished talking, we had dinner and me and Lucian went outside to talk about what had just happened.

"So, why didn't you tell me about the cure?" He didn't look at me when he said that. He just kept glancing to the side.

"Listen I'm really sorry I didn't tell you before. It just never came up in a conversation." I put my hand on his cheek and turned his face to look at me. "I never meant to make you feel left out or played. I'm really sorry."

He leaned down and kissed me. A soft, gentle kind of kiss that left you wanting more. When he went to pull away, I pulled him back towards me and what started as a gentle kiss turned into a passionate, hot kiss.

Before I knew it, I was pushed against the wall with my hands wrapped around his neck, pulling me closer to him. He lifted me off the ground, and my legs went directly around his waist. We stayed there for I don't know how long before I finally pulled away. We looked into each other's eyes as we traded breaths back and forth.

"I wish we could do this all night, but we have a guest inside and have to get an early start tomorrow." He let me go. As we went inside, I noticed that Casey had turned on the TV,, taken a shower and folded the couch out into a bed in the time we spent outside.

"Wow, that must have been one intense conversation. Here's a tip for you: Next time, close the curtains. I am still considered your legal dad, and I don't like seeing my children have make-out sessions through a window."

I don't know why, but I felt my cheeks grow warm.

"Yea, well, we also stay in the same bed, so you might as well get over it."

That night, while I lay in bed thinking about what was to come the next morning, I couldn't help but wonder what Jackson could be going through.

Chapter 10

Jackson

I keep having this recurring dream where Blake stabs me in the back and runs off with Lucian and the cure, but I know it's fake, and when I finally relieve myself of the dream, I see images of myself and everyone I know. I know it's me, and I'm doing the stuff I see, but I can't stop myself. I see and feel everything, and I hate myself for doing it. I remember before I started feeling this way that Thalia somehow got into my head and locked me out of my own head, which makes no sense... When did she get power? Before that day, Thalia didn't show any signs of powers or being anything other than human. I could feed off of her, and she never stopped us. So how?

"Oh, sweet Jackson, you know I can enter your mind whenever I want? You can't run or hide from me; neither can you hide your thoughts." She was in my head again. "If you really want to know how I'm able to do this, you could just ask; it's that simple."

"Okay, then how are you able to do this?"

"It's really simple. When you left with Blake and Lucian, your mom was outraged, and she knew that you would never trust her again, so she turned to me. She offered me strength and power if I got close to you and Blake. I was supposed to kill her and bring you home, but after she caught on to me, I had to change the plans a little. So instead, I took your mind and powers so that you could defeat Lucian and help capture Blake."

If I could make a confused face, I would, but then again, if I could do anything, I would go and find Blake

"That still doesn't answer how you got powers in the first place."

"Isn't it obvious? Your mom is feeding me power. It only makes sense that if y'all can take emotions and power, you can give them as well." She had a point. "Of course I do."

"So why did you need me to beat Lucian? Why not just use my mom's power to take Lucian. He was closer to Blake than I was at the time." I could feel the jealousy.

"Well, you see, I tried to do that the night Blake slept in his room, but Lucian had a barrier around both of them, and you trusted me more than they did."

"I should've listened to Blake when she told me not to trust you." The guilt hit me right in the face.

"Yeah, you should've, but you didn't, and now Blake and Lucian will die trying to get you back. I'll give you one thing though, you got good friends."

"Yeah, and they're going to ruin you and my mother."

"Maybe. I mean, they already took your father hostage. So, yeah, maybe they do have a chance at beating me and your mom. Plus the Blue Tiger Gang."

And with that, she left me to think by myself.

Chapter 11

Blake

I woke up in a cold sweat by myself. Casey and Lucian were gone. I was all alone, just like it was meant to be. I just sat down and waited to see whether they were going to come back or not. I waited there for three hours before they got back. Lucian came through the door in a rush to get to the bathroom, and Casey was right behind him carrying clothes from the house. I went rushing after Lucian to see what was wrong.

"What happened!" I was standing in the doorway watching him rinse him hands off in the sink. The water turned bright red.

"We went to the house to get the things, so we could go to the party and get Jackson back."

He turned to look at me, and he had a cut across his right cheek and eyebrow that was most definitely going to scar.

"Why didn't you wake me up? I could've helped."

He looked away from me out of guilt.

"We couldn't risk you getting caught again. You're the one part of the plan that is indispensable. You also needed your sleep."

I reached over and touched the cut across his face, and he winced.

"You need stitches."

"Yeah, I figured."

I left the room to go get some air while Casey stitched up Lucian's wound.

I had no idea how we were going to pull this off. It had been at least a month after Jackson was mind wiped or whatever had happened. How many people would be there, and could we really trust Casey? I had so many questions and doubts, but what scared me the most was that I'd been having this recurring feeling that we weren't all going to walk away from this. The only thing I could really do to make sure everyone I care about got home safe at the end of that night was too make sure that if anyone got hurt, it was be me.

That night, I couldn't really sleep. Every time I would fall asleep, even a little, I would dream of Lucian or Jackson dying. I've never cared for anyone because no one ever cared for me. Now that I did care about them, I couldn't lose them. I woke up the next day to breakfast sitting on the table. Casey and Lucian were outside waiting for me to get up probably. I got up and ate before going outside and seeing what they were talking about.

"What's going on out here?" I said in a humorous way. Lucian walked over and gave me a kiss on the forehead.

"Good morning, we were just discussing some of the details of how tomorrow is going to go."

"Oh… So, what did y'all come up with?" We walked back inside.

"So, we are going to wait till all of the guests show up, or at least enough to blend in a little. Then we will walk right in, and while you find Jackson and take him somewhere where Thalia and Julie aren't, we will find Thalia and put an end to Jackson's mind control."

"Not a bad plan, but what did you get for us to blend in exactly?"

He walked over to the pile of clothes sitting on a chair in the corner and pulled out my dress. The blue and white dress surprised me. I had totally forgotten about it.

"Wow, I had forgotten all about the dress."

"I figured it was probably the only dress you had, and we are running low on cash, so it was the most affordable." I took the dress in my hands, feeling the fabric. It was definitely expensive, no doubt about it.

"And tuxes for us, of course." He pulled the tux from the pile and laid it across the bed.

The rest of the day was spent planning and making sure we had all the details right, so nothing would go wrong. That night, Casey went to get food from a good restaurant across town because we decided if we were going to die tomorrow, we might as well enjoy our last meal. I looked over at Lucian, who was sitting on a chair in a corner of the room reading a book. I got off the couch I was sitting on, watching TV, and walked over to him. I grabbed the book gently from his hands and set it down on the table next to him. I put my legs on either sides of his and was sitting in his lap, which almost made me as tall as him.

"This is new. What would you like, dear?"

"I want you to promise me that no matter how dangerous a situation I get myself into, you won't try to save me." He looked at me and his eyebrows started to crease as he realized what I was asking.

"I can't promise you that. You know I can't." I could feel my eyes start to water.

"Please, Lucian, I just found people who care about me and who I care about. I can't lose you too." I could feel the tears roll down my face as I looked into his eyes.

"Blake… You're not going to lose me." He brushed the tears off my face with his thumb as he cupped my face in his hand.

"That's just it though, you know you can't promise me that." I put my hand on top of his, holding it there and feeling its warmth against my cheek. He looked into my eyes, and I could tell that he could feel my hurt, and he knew I was right.

"Okay, I promise I won't try to be a hero. Never thought I'd have to say that in my life."

I laughed, "You're not crossing your fingers, right?"

He held up his hands as proof, which made me laugh a little more. I sat there, looking into his eyes and then tried to stand up. He grabbed my waist and pulled me back down.

"You think you can come over here and sit in my lap, get me all hot and bothered, and then just leave like that?"

Actually, that was exactly what I'd thought.

"Uhh… Yeah…?"

He gave me a mischievous smile and shook his head.

"Not how it works, doll." He pulled me against him and pulled me in for a kiss. Before he could kiss me, I flipped my body to where I was now sitting in his lap. He laughed at that.

"You think that's going to stop me?" He moved my hair away from my neck and kissed me. The kiss sent shivers down my spine making me breathe really heavily. I felt a smile spread across my lips.

"Lucian, don't leave any marks, or I'll kill you!"

He pulled away and turned my head towards his.

"Well, maybe if someone would have given me a kiss, I wouldn't have to leave my mark on her."

"Oh really." I pushed our lips together, which sent sparks through my body, which led to more than just lips when we kissed. We somehow ended up on the bed, and I started pulling off his shirt, trying to get more and more of him. At some point, my shirt came off before Lucian finally pulled away.

"Lucian? What the hell? Now who's leaving who hot and bothered."

He laughed and sat beside me on the bed.

"We both know that we have to get enough sleep for tomorrow, and that Casey will be here any minute. Plus, I don't want to do this here. It's not that I don't want you. It's just that I think we should do this when we are both absolutely sure, and when we aren't worried about what'll happen in the future. I want us to be able to handle the consequences of our actions."

I could see where he was coming from. I put my shirt back on and laid there with him, waiting for the food. I put my head on his chest and listened to his heart beat while holding his head. We ended up falling asleep because the food never got there.

Chapter 12

Lucian

That morning, Blake woke me up, frantic as ever. Apparently, Casey never came back with food last night.

"I don't know how we are going to do this. What if he stabbed us in the back and told them our plan? How are we going to get there? He took your car!"

I walked over to her and put my hand on her shoulder getting her to look at me.

"Everything will be fine, I promise. We can just rent a car for tonight and figure the rest out. This is our only chance." I leaned down and kissed her cheek, trying to make her feel a little better. She took a deep breath and started walking towards the bathroom. "What are you doing?" I asked.

"Uhh… Going to the bathroom to get ready for tonight. It's already three in the afternoon. We overslept." She gave me a cute smile and closed the door.

I started getting my things laid out on the bed and went to the mirror by the side of the bathroom to brush my teeth and gel my hair. After I shaved and my hair was fixed, I started getting dressed. When I reached for my tux, I realized that Casey's tux was gone, which meant that he knew he wasn't going to be coming back last night. I decided not to tell Blake because it would only make her freak out more than she already was.

When I was finally putting my socks and shoes on, Blake walked out of the bathroom. She had her hair tied up in a bun with side bangs and curly strands hanging out on the sides of her face. The dress fit her figure perfectly. The top was tight and hung to her curves while the bottom flowed out; it was beautiful. She had the smallest amount of lipstick and mascara on.

"You're gorgeous." I was awestruck.

"Thanks, you look great, too." I had stopped putting my shoes on and had to resume while she put her flats on. I was going to get her heels, but then I figured that it would be nice if she could actually be active in the footwear.

"Are you nervous about how tonight will go?" She looked at me worried.

"A little, but everything will be fine, I'll use my barrier to make sure they can't tell you're human." We were waiting on the car that I had called to come get us when Blake ran back upstairs to get something that she left. By the time she came back down, the car was there, and I was waiting for her with the door open. She climbed into the car, and I went after her.

"What did you forget?" She pulled up the skirt of her dress revealing a knife in a holster on her thigh.

"Well, okay then." I laughed.

After about an hour in the car, we started to see all the cars and lights from the celebration. There were over 300 people at the house that we could see. Most of the people were dressed in really fancy, really expensive clothes. It made sense though because Jackson's family had been there for a really long time, building their connections to the community and places around it. We got out of the car and paid the cab. Before walking any closer to the house, I stopped Blake.

"We need to stick together until we find Jackson and them, okay? Don't wander off on your own!" She looked at me then smiled.

"When have I ever done that?" Wow, she was really joking at a time like this. She saw that I wasn't smiling. "Listen, we have to at least play it off that we are just guests. We can't have serious faces the whole night." She had a point.

"Okay, well, I'll spread my barrier to you, and we can go." We started walking towards the house and saw my car parked out front.

"So, he did come back here. Do you think he told them about the plan?" She asked me through the mental link.

"I honestly don't know."

We were walking into the house. In the big entryway, there were tables by the wall decorated with blue flowers and white table cloths. The chandelier was cleaned off, glowing with a sparkling yellow and white light. The floor

70

was polished, and there were many couples dancing to the music the band on the stage was playing.

"May I have this dance?" I bowed and held out my hand to Blake.

"You may." She smiled and grabbed my hand.

Chapter 13

Blake

As we danced together, we both searched for Jackson or anyone else. There was a loud sound, like a trumpet. Everyone stopped dancing and looked at the top of the stairs where Jackson and Thalia walked down the stairs arm-in-arm. Thalia was wearing a blue to purple dress that fell down to her feet and was strapless. Thalia's hair was pinned back in a bun, and she had black eyeliner that made her blue eyes pop. Jackson had a black and white tux on with a blue lilac tucked into his jacket. He had his hair slicked back and a nice tie on, but his eyes had no emotion. I couldn't help but feel a little twinge of jealousy. Lucian looked down at me, probably wondering what that feeling was.

When Jackson and Thalia reached the bottom of the stairs, Julie and Casey began to walk down the stairs. Julie had a red dress with a flower embroidered corset top, which was also strapless. Her hair was straightened, and Casey had the same tux as his son, but with a rose in the pocket on the jacket. Julie and Casey stopped halfway down the stairs.

"Thank you all for coming. I know it was a very long drive for some, but it was worth it. It has been too long since we've had a gathering. Most of you think that you've come all this way for a simple celebration of how long our family has been here, but actually we are celebrating my sons coming home. We have had some issues with a hunter this year, but he finally came back to us." Casey looked at us and…

Winked! He literally winked at us! What was that supposed to mean?!

"We are also celebrating the engagement of my son, Jackson, and his future wife, Thalia."

Everything froze when I heard that. It was unbelievable. I didn't even realize I had taken a step forward until Lucian grabbed my hand to hold me back.

"Blake, calm down. We will put an end to this tonight, I promise," he told me through the mental link. I had been trying to burn the mental link when he told me that because I could feel the heat coming off of Lucian. As soon as Julie stopped talking, everyone started talking and dancing again. Me and Lucian went and sat at a table far away from Julie and them.

"So how are we going to get their attention?" We both looked at each other and then looked at Jackson.

"I'm going to go and get Thalia away from Jackson while you get Jackson to follow you outside, away from the crowd. Then I will somehow manage to knock Thalia unconscious, so you can break Jackson free somehow."

I nodded and watched as Lucian stood up and walked over to Thalia and Jackson. Lucian bowed over and took Thalia's hand, as if asking her to dance. I felt a little bit of hurt strike me, but I knew he didn't want her, so I brushed it off. I started walking towards Jackson when he finally spotted me, and I started walking towards the door that led to the yard.

I hoped Jackson was following me and that he was alone. I finally got to a place that no one was around, and I turned to see if Jackson had followed. He did…

But so did Julie.

"Why am I not surprised that you would be here to ruin this?" Julie walked right next to Jackson and set her hand on his shoulder, which made me mad.

"The only reason you're doing this is because you want to trap him into the family," I snapped back.

"I can't deny that reasoning, but actually, it's to keep him from going off with you." That sent shock up my spine. Jackson doesn't like me.

I felt the mental link start to shrink, and then it stopped. I hoped Lucian wasn't having any trouble.

"It's done," Lucian said through the link.

"Okay, I'm out in the garden." Then the link settled back down and disappeared. I looked up at Julie and Jackson, who were both the same as before Lucian knocked out Thalia.

"You really think that I wouldn't know that you and Lucian are aiming at Thalia? I took the mental link between her and Jackson off and switched it to me instead."

Julie had a wild smirk on her face that I really wanted to knock off. I started walking toward her, and for every step I took, Jackson took two. He started running toward me. He was three feet away when he pulled back for a punch and swung at me. I ducked underneath the punch and kicked his leg out from under him. He fell to the ground, and I put my knee on his chest. I swung at him trying to knock him out, but he rolled out from underneath me, sending me off balance and making me punch the hard ground.

He stood up and drove his knee at my face. It slammed into my jaw, sending me spiraling toward the ground. I caught myself and stood up before he could do anymore. He swung at my face again, but this time, I grabbed his wrist and threw him over my shoulder. While he was down, I lunged at Julie. I sprinted probably 30 feet before even getting close to her when Jackson tackled me to the ground. He reached under my dress and unclipped the knife from my upper thigh sending shivers up my spine. He placed the edge of the knife against my throat. I looked into his lifeless eyes and silently pleaded, trying to find any sign that he was still in there, but he didn't even look around.

"You're not going to be able to get through to him. Mainly because I am controlling what he does. Jackson hasn't ever had the willpower to do much of anything."

Jackson didn't even react to the insult.

"Kill her," Julie said with no emotion. Jackson didn't move. "I said kill her!" Julie yelled this time, and beads of sweat started rolling down her forehead. Then she smiled, and Jackson started pushing the knife against my throat, and I felt the warmth of blood roll down the side of my neck. Black spots started forming in my vision.

Just when I thought I was going to pass out and everything would be over, Lucian flew across my view and tackled Jackson to the ground. I got up and stumbled around looking for the knife. My vision swayed; I couldn't find the knife, so I decided my best bet was to just go after Julie.

I turned to lunge at Julie but stopped mid-run. Philip was standing between me and Julie, looking as emotionless as before.

"Please, son, don't let her near your dear old mother," Julie whimpered like a coward.

Philip just nodded at his mother's request. I could feel the energy from my willpower being drained slowly. I took a step forward, and it felt like I was wading through mud. I stopped and allowed myself to sink into Philip's manipulation. I took a deep breath and ripped back out of the mind link. Philip screamed out and fell to the ground curling into a ball.

"How could you do that?" Julie fell to the ground, holding her son as he sobbed.

"Time to rid this world of you." I didn't feel any emotion; I only felt the hatred for Julie and her wicked ways. "Julie, I condemn you to death for crimes against the human race and the Shaitan community."

I wrapped my hand around Julie's neck and squeezed as hard as I could. When I heard the snap of her neck and saw the life drain from her eyes, I released her body to fall limp on the ground. I heard a wailing behind me and turned to see what it was. What I saw felt like a smack to the face. Jackson was standing over Lucian, about to drive the knife into his chest.

"What! Oh my God, I'm so sorry!" Jackson fell over and laid his head on his knees. I ran over to Lucian. I was looking him up and down.

"Are you okay?" I placed my hand on his cheek. He put his hand over mine and studied me, probably checking if I was okay.

"Yes, I'm fine. You might want to check on him though." He looked at Jackson, who was still sitting in the same position and sobbing. He reminded me of Philip, who was gone. I walked over to Jackson and wrapped my arms around him. He leaned into me.

"I'm so sorry. I should have believed you when you said something about Thalia." He looked into my eyes, and I could see the internal damage that his mother did to him. "I can't believe I couldn't stop myself. I didn't have the power." He looked at my throat, which had stopped bleeding but left a trail of blood running down my chest.

"We forgive you. None of what you did was your fault."

Lucian walked over and slapped Jackson on the shoulder.

"Come on, dude, that was the best fight we've ever had. I actually had competition this time."

Jackson laughed a little. Lucian helped us up. We started walking back to the house, and I grabbed Lucian's hand.

"Excuse me, when did that happen?" Jackson looked shocked and pointed at Lucian's hand in mine. I had forgotten that the last time he really saw us was when he was pissed off because I slept in Lucian's room.

"A lot has happened." I said, smiling while looking at Lucian. We were almost to the house when Thalia came barreling out of the door.

"Jackson, kill them!" Thalia screamed and pointed at me and Lucian. Jackson looked at her then shook his head.

"I don't take orders from anyone anymore, and you no longer have abilities." She looked stunned by his words. She put her head down and started to shake. Then she started laughing and reached behind her.

"If you wouldn't have distracted me, none of this would have happened." She drew out a gun and pointed it at Lucian. Right when I saw the gun everything went in slow motion. Jackson went one way while i jumped towards Lucian. Thalia pulled the trigger, and pain surged up my body. Jackson tackled Thalia and held her down. People came rushing outside, and Jackson yelled at someone to call the police and the ambulance.

Lucian was kneeling beside me struggling to control the bleeding.

"Blake, stay with me. Don't close your eyes. Please, you promised me you wouldn't do anything stupid. You said you wouldn't be the hero."

Tears fell down his cheeks and landed on mine.

"I couldn't just let her kill you. I love you Lucian."

Jackson sat down beside me and grabbed my hand.

"The ambulance is 30 minutes away. Blake, I just got you back. I can't lose you again."

I looked up at both of them and for once I was okay with dying because it was for the people I love. I put my hand on top of where Lucian was putting pressure on my stomach.

"It's okay. I'm so glad I got to have y'all in my life, even if it was for… Only a little…"

Blood started dripping down my cheek from my mouth, and finally, the coldness settled over me…

And everything went blank.